D1287685

THE BRINK OF FAME

ALSO BY IRENE FLEMING

The Edge of Ruin

THE BRINK OF FAME

IRENE FLEMING

MINOTAUR BOOKS
NEW YORK

This is a work of fiction. All of the characters, organizations, and events portrayed in this novel are either products of the author's imagination or are used fictitiously.

THE BRINK OF FAME. Copyright © 2011 by Kathleen Dunn. All rights reserved. Printed in the United States of America. For information, address St. Martin's Press, 175 Fifth Avenue, New York, N.Y. 10010.

www.minotaurbooks.com

Book design by Rich Arnold

Library of Congress Cataloging-in-Publication Data

Fleming, Irene, 1939–
    The brink of fame / Irene Fleming.—1st ed.
        p.   cm.
    ISBN 978-0-312-57544-1
    1. Abandoned wives—Fiction.   2. Motion picture
producers and directors—Fiction.   3. Women
detectives—Fiction.   4. Missing persons—Investigation—
Fiction.   5. Actors—Crimes against—Fiction.
6. Hollywood (Los Angeles, Calif.)—Fiction.   I. Title.

    PS3557.A414B75 2011
    813'.54—dc22

                                    2011009100

First Edition: August 2011

10 9 8 7 6 5 4 3 2 1

For Liz Donovan, my sister

THE BRINK OF FAME

ONE

When Emily Daggett Weiss boarded the Twentieth Century Limited in the spring of 1914, bound for a brief sojourn in the West, one or two old biddies gave her the hairy eye. Woman traveling alone. No better than she should be, as her mother used to say about young women of low moral standards. Worse than the biddies, a traveling salesman winked at her.

Her attire was sober and dignified, a charcoal traveling suit and pearl gray kid gloves, auburn hair tucked out of sight under a fairly quiet hat, lined in French crepe and sparingly trimmed with ostrich pom-poms. She hadn't worked as a chorus girl for a good five years, not since she and Adam were married, not since they became successful movie producers. She was the most powerful woman in

Fort Lee, New Jersey, film capital of the world, and still strangers were thinking bad things about her because she was by herself on a train.

Turning away from them, she opened a newspaper on her lap. Between five and ten thousand suffragettes were marching on Washington for women's rights. The train started up with a shudder. Emily would have said she had all the rights she would ever need, other than the vote, in a brand-new twentieth-century industry where women were considered the equals of men. It was she who ran Melpomene Moving Picture Studios, hiring and firing, selling and purchasing, while Adam, her husband and business partner, took care of the creative end of things.

Their partnership had created a multimillion-dollar empire whose studio occupied many acres of prime Fort Lee real estate. Their business and their marriage were the envy of their flighty show-business friends. And yet . . .

The train emerged from its tunnel into a gray morning, rainy and chilly. Emily looked at herself in the rain-streaked window, straightened her hat, rearranged the pins in her hair, and searched her reflected face for signs of anxiety. Something wasn't right.

Adam had set off for Flagstaff, Arizona, the week before. Someone had told him that Flagstaff was in the desert. His plan was to film an Arabian extravaganza with camels and tents. He told Emily he would see about the camels when he got there.

Emily was to meet him on location after she tied up a few loose ends in Fort Lee. "We'll only be separated for a week," he said.

But a cold, clammy feeling of something not right pervaded the studios in Fort Lee. The more she explained to Melpomene's employees that it was all the thing nowadays to make a moving picture on location, that she and Mr. Weiss would be back in no time at all, the more false warmth they put into their assent. Of course, Mrs. Weiss, don't give it a thought, naturally Mr. Weiss must go to Flagstaff and take his leading actress. As she went out the door they shook her hand or hugged her good-bye and then looked searchingly into her eyes, as if she were leaving Fort Lee forever, as if she had a terminal illness and had not yet been told. The last one to know.

In Chicago Emily changed trains for the California Limited, the pride of the Santa Fe line. She settled her head on the embroidered antimacassar of the Pullman lounge seat and opened a fresh newspaper to survey the latest happenings. While the train was hurtling into the West, it seemed that Woodrow Wilson was declaring this day to be Mother's Day, as a sop to the voteless women. But national politics was not interesting to her. Her attention was consumed by a nameless dread. The flat gray countryside flew away behind her, scarcely noticed. She slept badly in her shaky Pullman berth and picked at her food in the rocking, swaying dining car.

Then as the train chugged into Arizona Emily's mood began to lift. The western sun streamed in the windows. The world seemed a better place. Flagstaff was mere hours away now. In Flagstaff, Adam had told her, the sun shone every day, no waiting for favorable weather before you could shoot a motion picture. Not like Fort Lee. When at last she joined him at the Weatherford Hotel, the finest ac-commodations to be had in Flagstaff, or so he said, she would lose all her feelings of unease in Adam's warm arms. They would go out and look for camels together.

Just over the Arizona border the train slowed and stopped in Coronado Junction, with a great hissing of steam, shrieking of brakes, and banging together of couplings. On the station platform stood a tall man in tweeds and a derby hat, carrying a Gladstone bag. He looked up at the window of the train and saw Emily looking back at him. At once he recognized her. He beamed with surprise and delight; in seconds he was aboard her very car. Holbert Bruns.

Holbert Bruns, detective, man of mystery, faintly Great Dane–like, whose hooded eyes and pendulous lower lip appeared sometimes in Emily's erotic dreams. Well, you can't help what you dream. Emily had nothing to reproach herself for. She was faithful to Adam in every other re-spect, and as for the dream about Holbert Bruns in the Paris taxicab, she always forgot about it the instant she woke up. Bruns as a flesh-and-blood human being was more un-settling than erotic, chiefly because he could not be trusted to tell the truth. Nothing he had ever said to her was true. She wished he hadn't boarded this train. Still, she couldn't quite bring herself to scream at him to go away when he sat down next to her on the Pullman seat. For one thing it would create an unpleasant scene.

"Mrs. Weiss! What a delightful surprise."

"Mr. Bruns."

"What brings you to the West?"

"Mr. Weiss and I are going to make a moving picture together."

"I see. And does he still force you to climb out and dangle on the edge of cliffs for the sake of making pictures?"

"Do you still burn up irreplaceable historical documents for the sake of the Pinkertons?"

"I don't work for the Pinkertons anymore," Bruns said. "Anything I burn, I burn for my own sake." He took out a pipe and filled it with fragrant tobacco.

She narrowed her eyes at him.

"It's true, Mrs. Weiss. I left the Pinkertons last year, and since then I have been in business for myself."

"Are you on a case?"

"Always. Always on a case." He scratched a match on the sole of his boot, held it to the bowl of his pipe, sucked at the pipe stem. A cloud of smoke formed around them.

"What sort of case?" she said.

He smiled. "Always confidential."

"Won't you tell me?"

"The current case involves a missing person; that's all I can tell you."

"But to beguile an idle hour, Mr. Bruns, surely . . ."

He looked her in the eyes and laughed. "You must be bored indeed."

"Yes, I am. I've read all the newspapers and magazines I bought in Chicago. But on top of that I'm curious about the work you do. Perhaps you can tell me, in general terms, how one goes about finding a missing person, without betraying any confidences."

He puffed on the straight black stem of his pipe. The

bowl—round, brown, gleaming—glowed red inside. Emily noticed that Bruns's thumbnail was clean and well-trimmed but not professionally manicured. More clouds of smoke enveloped them.

"In general, then, the technique is to discover as much as possible about the person who is said to be missing. Who says this person is missing? That's the first question."

"Presumably, the one who is paying you to find this person says he is missing," Emily said.

"Quite so. But to himself, he may not be missing, if you get my drift."

"Oh, I do. And of course you would work with local law enforcement officers."

He gave her a long stare, perhaps attempting to determine whether she was trying to be funny. "Not in these parts, Mrs. Weiss. There is no law west of the Pecos, at least none worthy of the name."

"I see."

"So, to continue. I would find out what makes my client think the subject is missing. Then I would determine what the subject's habits are, who his friends are, and incidentally whether they, too, believe he is missing. Sometimes this involves a certain amount of surveillance."

Emily jotted a few words in her pocket notebook. "Spy on the man's friends. Right."

"Of course. They could be hiding him. Say, are you writing a book?"

"I thought I might make a moving picture. Then what?"

"Then I look for the subject's assets. People have to eat. I find out whether he has put money or valuables away, where he might have put them, whether he has touched them after he went missing. If he hasn't—well, then I begin to suspect foul play."

"Foul play." She noted it down.

"Yes."

"So you're putting a lot of effort into your case right now."

"It's keeping me busy. As for you, Mrs. Weiss, I hear you've been busy yourself, doing good works."

"Good works?"

"Yes. They say you saved Flo Ziegfeld's marriage to Billie Burke last month."

"That was nothing," Emily said. "Miss Burke stopped by our studio in Fort Lee, and I gave her a bouquet of flowers to take to Mr. Ziegfeld on the steamship."

He smirked, if a Great Dane could be said to smirk. "That's not the way I heard it."

"Do tell. I wonder where you heard it."

"Mrs. Weiss, my field of inquiry is the moving picture business. I hear many things."

"People will always be talking."

"So the story about the steamer trunk . . . ?"

"Just a story." She shrugged. "I believe in marriage, Mr. Bruns. I believe that married couples owe each other fidelity."

"Ah," he said. Of course Bruns had heard that speech from Emily on another occasion, years ago in Fort Lee, when he tried to get her to leave Adam and run away with him to Nebraska. Still, it was important to her to make the point again, especially with him sitting so close to her, the warmth of his left leg somehow penetrating her gabardine skirt and two silk petticoats. She moved away from him slightly and thought about the incident with Billie Burke.

It happened on the second to the last day of shooting for *Divine Retribution*. Agnes Gelert, Melpomene Pictures' only big-name female star, was emoting for the camera after her fashion; Emily was working behind her desk in her office. The days of anonymous movie actors were past and gone. No more were the principal actresses in studio films known to the moviegoing public only as the Vitagraph Girl, or the Biograph Girl, not since the lovely Florence Lawrence left Biograph for Carl Laemmle's IMP in 1910 for a chance to have her own name up on the movie screen. After that, all the popular actors and actresses demanded to be known, and to be well paid for being known. And the public demanded to know them, even to know, as far as possible, the details of their darlings' private lives.

Many studios in the modern day employed publicity people to invent these details. Melpomene did not, not yet, and so when a woman arrived at the studio and identified herself as a reporter from *Photoplay* magazine who wanted to do a feature on Agnes Gelert (formerly known as the Melpomene Girl), Emily told the receptionist to show her into her office.

The Melpomene Girl's real private life would have horrified most of her fans. Emily herself had made up some harmless (if false) details, summarized in a prepared handout, which she forced Miss Gelert to parrot to reporters as a condition of continued employment.

The rowdy Miss Gelert was Melpomene's most valuable star in spite of her off-camera behavior. The camera loved her eyes, enormous and haunting, her rosebud lips, all freshness, innocence, and fun, and her figure, so slim and graceful. The silent screen did not reveal her grating voice or vulgar utterances to the moviegoing public. Why should Emily let them know what she was really like?

The reporter who came into Emily's office wore a brown scratchy-looking tweed walking suit, horribly unbecoming, a dowdy hat, drab kid gloves, wire-rimmed pince-nez eyeglasses, and no makeup whatsoever, not a trace. Still, there was something remarkably attractive about her face, an almost feverish sparkle in her blue eyes that the glasses could not conceal.

"Miss Gelert is busy on the set right now," Emily said to her, "but I'm sure she can talk to you as soon as she finishes filming this scene. Meanwhile, perhaps you'd like some tea." She lit the gas ring and put a kettle on to boil. "While you wait I can tell you some things about Miss Gelert's life. For example, she was born in the town of Michigan City, Indiana, where her father was a Baptist minister. Do sit down." Emily gestured toward the sofa, upholstered in plum-colored silk, one of the many touches indicating that this was a woman's office.

"Yes, yes," the reporter said. "All of that is well known. What I want to ask her about today is her liaison with Florenz Ziegfeld." She drew a pencil and a stenographer's notebook from her smart leather handbag. Emily glimpsed inside the heavy bag a mother-of-pearl cigarette case. Or, it might have been the handle of a pistol.

"Ziegfeld, the impresario?" How had this person heard

about Agnes and Ziegfeld? Nobody knew about that. If the story came out it would mean ruin, not only for Agnes but for Melpomene Studios as well. "There is no liaison. Mr. Ziegfeld may have taken a fatherly interest in Miss Gelert a few years ago, when she was dancing in his Midnight Frolics. Why, Agnes is barely nineteen." In fact the girl was twenty-six, but nineteen was the official studio figure. "Mr. Ziegfeld must be—oh, I don't know—"

"Forty-seven," the reporter murmured.

"And he's a married man now, married to Miss Billie Burke, herself a famous star of the stage." Emily took two porcelain cups and saucers out of her desk drawer.

The reporter's eyes, blue as sapphires, flashed behind the pince-nez. "So you are not aware that Miss Gelert and Mr. Ziegfeld plan to sail away to Europe this evening on the *Mauretania*."

"That can't be true," Emily said. "Miss Gelert has to be here tomorrow to finish filming *Divine Retribution*."

The reporter laughed with scorn, a high, tinkling laugh. "Mrs. Weiss, you are naïve to expect Miss Gelert to respect any obligations she may have to your studio. It is my understanding that Miss Gelert fears neither God nor man." It dawned on Emily that this person was Billie Burke herself, heavily but not impenetrably disguised. With the firearm in her handbag she clearly meant to threaten Agnes Gelert, or worse.

"Ah, the teakettle," Emily said, and busied herself with tea balls and preparations. While Miss Burke peered anxiously through the glass door and out into the studio, no doubt seeking to draw a bead on Agnes, Emily stirred a sleeping powder into the woman's tea. "One lump or two?"

"Two, please. And a little milk."

"You might as well be comfortable," Emily said. "Miss Gelert will be another fifteen or twenty minutes. Here, put this pillow behind your head. I embroidered it myself." Half a cup would be enough to put a woman of Miss Burke's size and weight to sleep for several hours; Emily watched her as she drank it down. "Would you like a digestive biscuit?"

"Thank you, no. I'm watching my figure," Miss Burke said, and sank further into the sofa with a sigh. Behind the wire pince-nez the beautiful lashes fluttered shut.

Emily covered Miss Burke with a paisley shawl and then went straight to Agnes Gelert's dressing room. There her worst fears were confirmed. A steamer trunk stood packed and ready, labeled for the stateroom of Florenz Ziegfeld aboard the *Mauretania*. She rushed out into the studio. Agnes was still in the arms of Harley Crowther, visibly suffering the pangs of movie fate while the film director screamed at her and the camera rolled. Ed Eardley, Melpomene's aged prop boy, stood watching the scene, a brace and bit dangling from his arthritic fingers.

"Psst! Ed!" Emily beckoned to him. "Is your cousin Frank still looking for work?"

"Sure is."

"Can he be here in two minutes?"

"Sure can."

She told Ed what she wanted his cousin to do. "And let me have that, please. I have some holes to bore." Back in

Agnes's dressing room, she took the brace and bit and began to ventilate the steamer trunk. It wasn't long before Agnes appeared in the doorway.

"Why are you boring holes in my luggage?"

"I'm afraid I can't approve of your plans to leave Fort Lee before you finish this picture."

"And you're gonna sink my trunk? You can't keep me here, you know, Mrs. Weiss." She took off her movie costume and threw it on the floor. "It's a free country. Lincoln freed the slaves, in case you hadn't hoid."

"Did he? How interesting," Emily said.

Agnes smeared her face with cold cream and began to towel it off. "The *Mauretania* sails in two hours, and I mean to be on it."

"Why don't you take the studio limousine?"

"So your driver can run me to Trenton and back while the ship sails without me? I'll be sure and do that, I *don't* think."

Emily squatted back on her heels and surveyed her work. Twelve neat holes, each half an inch in diameter. "There, that ought to be enough."

"I get it." Agnes inspected her face in the mirror and reapplied a little powder and lip rouge. "You think you're going to lock me up in my own trunk until after the ship sails." She slipped into a flowered street dress, one arm at a time, wiggling.

"That would be foolish of me, wouldn't it?"

"I'll say it would. I'm not completely green, you know."

"A pity. Now let's open up this steamer trunk and make sure I didn't damage any of your clothes."

"You open it up." Agnes tossed her the key. "And I'd better not find out you stole anything. Mr. Ziegfeld's man will be here any minute to pick up my things; you can give him that key. As for me, I'm getting away from here before you try something funny."

"I don't do comedy, Agnes."

"Ha-ha. Well, neither do I. I'm seriously getting out of this lousy studio. I can't stand woiking for you another five minutes, you and your rules about the clean life and your fake stories about me. Why should I be ashamed of who I am? Who cares how old I am, for instance? Who cares whether I like to take a drink now and then, or who I choose to spend my time with?" Hurrying now, she did up the buttons of her dress. "Or whether I show up at this stinking studio or not. Once, just once, I want to sleep past eight o'clock without people yelling at me."

"Won't you miss your dinner?"

"Shut up, Mrs. Weiss. Just shut up. You think you're smotter than me just because you married a rich guy."

"No, I think I'm smarter than you because you're stupider than me."

"We'll just see about that. It just so happens that I'm deeply in love with Flo Ziegfeld. Who happens to be rich, richer than Adam Weiss, rich enough to buy you and sell you and your stupid contract."

"And who also happens to be married."

"So what? And let me tell you something else. If I find out you got shavings all over my best clothes you'll hear from Mr. Ziegfeld's lawyers." She jammed a hat on her head.

"Miss Gelert, you have a contractual obligation to be

here tomorrow morning at seven to finish this moving picture."

"Sue me." She grabbed her handbag and gloves.

"I'll do better than that. I'll kick your hind end up between your ears."

She backed through the door. "You wouldn't dare."

"No? Watch me."

"Mr. Ziegfeld's man will come for my luggage," Agnes said, still backing up. "Good-bye, Mrs. Weiss. Don't think it hasn't been fun, because it hasn't." She turned and rushed out of the studio, right through the front lobby and into a waiting cab.

It was Melpomene's trusty receptionist who helped Emily unpack the steamer trunk, select Agnes's prettiest dress, and wrestle it onto the unconscious form of Billie Burke. When the man came to take the trunk to Ziegfeld's stateroom on the *Mauretania,* Miss Burke was attractively nestled inside it among Emily's pillows, still fast asleep. How could Ziegfeld resist her? How could he think of the trashy Agnes, with his own fair wife in front of him? The cab outside the studio that Agnes boarded in her haste was a movie prop driven by Ed Eardley's cousin Frank, who had instructions to drive her to Trenton and back and deliver her to the studio at seven the next morning.

When Agnes did arrive at the studio the next morning, exactly on time, for a change, Emily fully expected her to throw a fit. They were all used to her fits. Instead of that, she gave Emily a long, cool stare and got straight to work. In fact she acquitted herself so well that Adam promised her the leading role in his Arabian epic, and the following week the two of them took off for Flagstaff.

Once again proving that all's well that ends well.

Yes, there were flowers involved, three camellias, to be exact. Emily placed them in Miss Burke's lovely bosom before closing the trunk. She also took the liberty of lifting the gun from Miss Burke's handbag. She had it with her still; a woman never knows when she might need a pearl-handled revolver.

TWO

The dusty windows of the California Limited were streaked with rain by the time they pulled into the station in Flagstaff. Holbert Bruns offered to escort Emily as far as her hotel.

"No thank you, Mr. Bruns," she said. "Now that I'm here in Flagstaff I can confidently place myself under the protection of my husband." She looked out of the streaky window. Adam did not appear to be on the station platform. Carefully holding her skirt, she stepped down off the train and went in search of her bags, as Holbert Bruns strode off in the direction of the main street of town with his Gladstone bag in his hand. Oh, to be a man, Emily thought fleetingly, and travel light. A porter unloaded her things from the baggage car onto a big-wheeled cart.

"Where is the sun? I thought it shone all the time here. Where is the desert?" she asked the porter. Flagstaff looked nothing like a Western movie set. It was too built up, although blurry gray mountains loomed over the town in an interesting way, and a few stray cowboys and Indians huddled in the shelter of storefronts. How could anyone make a movie here? There wasn't even a tree to hang the outlaws. Fort Lee back east had more to offer.

"This is the desert," the porter said. "Only sometimes it rains. Been raining three days now." Things looked bad for Adam's desert epic. He was surely holed up at the hotel, striving to amuse himself, with no company other than the vapid Agnes Gelert, and maybe his elusive silent partner, Howie Kazanow.

Emily tipped the porter, checked her bags with the station's baggage clerk, and set off for the Weatherford Hotel, two blocks away. Who could have guessed how badly she would need an umbrella, here in this so-called desert? Her saucy hat was beginning to droop. But Adam would be waiting and would provide her with tea and sandwiches. Perhaps she would at last meet the mysterious Howie. Adam had mentioned that Howie was coming from California to Flagstaff to see him. Too bad she looked like a drowned rat for their first meeting.

The interior of the Weatherford Hotel smelled of wet wool and sheep manure, with a subtle undertone of bay rum that seemed to be emanating from a group of slick-looking men gathered at the far end of the lobby. None of them was Adam. At the desk Emily inquired after her husband.

"Who?"

"Mr. Adam Weiss."

The clerk put his pimply nose to the guest register, squinting, turning the pages one by one. "We had a Mr. and Mrs. Adam Weiss here, but they checked out yesterday evening," he said finally.

"There has to be some mistake."

"Can't help it, lady."

"I'm sorry. I must be in the wrong hotel," Emily said. "Excuse me." She moved away from the desk and sat down to think. Either she was in the wrong hotel or Adam was registered under an assumed name for reasons of his own. A drop of water, and then another, fell from the ostrich pom-pom onto Emily's good gray skirt. The dye was running. She rubbed it with her gloved hand. Maybe Adam thought Thomas Edison and his Trust detectives were after him again. Yes, that would account for it. He was registered under an assumed name. Or he was staying at another hotel. How many hotels were there in Flagstaff?

The chair where she was sitting and collecting herself was backed up against a sofa. Some man on the sofa emitted a braying laugh, breaking Emily's train of thought. She glanced over her shoulder to see two men, the quiet one apparently a traveling salesman, and the other a very sharply dressed . . . no telling what he was.

"The schmuck lost it to me in a poker game," said the sharp one. "Can you beat that? Ha-ha! You'd think he would have learned in college not to challenge me at poker. I never lose. So I am now the sole owner of Melpomene Moving Picture Studios."

"I guess congratulations are in order, Mr. Kazanow,"

the salesman said. "I'll certainly think a long time before I play poker with you."

So this was Howie Kazanow, Adam's childhood friend and longtime adversary. Emily had always hated him, even though they had never met. He hung over her marriage to Adam like a sword, threatening to fall on them every time they made an economic misstep. And yet Adam refused to disentangle his finances from this person's; like some sick gambler, he kept saying that this time, this time for sure, he would get the better of Howie Kazanow.

Nowadays Kazanow was Adam's West Coast silent partner, having invested heavily in Melpomene over Emily's objections. Adam kept telling her that Howie was scouting out a place in California for them to build another studio. But in the partnership was an element of risk that Adam had never adequately explained to her. Sometimes Adam would tell her that she would have to do better in this way or that way, business-wise, or else Howie Kazanow would come and take it all; what he meant by that, he would never say. It seemed from what Kazanow was saying now that Adam had finally got into a struggle with him that he couldn't win.

A poker game? How was this possible? Now that Emily saw his face—his smug, full lips, his needle nose, his beetling yellow brows—her hatred for Howie Kazanow matured and blossomed. At that moment she hated this man so much that it was causing her to feel faint.

"The first thing I'll do is tell that trollop wife of his to get out of my studio and go back to the kitchen where she belongs. If she even has a kitchen to go back to. Ha-ha-ha.

He left her, did you hear about that? Sneaked out of town as soon as he signed everything over to me. They say she was supposed to meet him here."

"Is Mrs. Weiss a trollop, then?" the drummer asked mildly.

"She used to be a chorus girl. They're all trollops."

The last drop of blood drained out of Emily's head. The room turned black. She leaned forward and put her head between her knees, hoping that people would think she was adjusting the buttons on her shoes, and tried to breathe deeply. Chuckling together, the two men rose from the sofa with a twanging of upholstery springs and walked away. One of them left behind a strong hair tonic smell.

When the blackness passed off, Emily stood up. Touching pieces of furniture for balance, leaning on the wall, she made her way as best she could to the ladies' lounge. Before the long mirror where the ladies were expected to primp stood five backless upholstered stools, relics of the days of bustles. Emily sat down on one of them, put her head in her hands, and wept.

Presently she felt a hand patting her back. She took one last shuddering, gasping sob and looked up. A woman stood over her—dark-haired, handsome, lightly rouged, wearing kid gloves and a hat trimmed in leghorn and pheasant feathers, a better hat than Emily's. She leaned on a walking stick, although Emily would have said she was too young to need one.

The woman's face was all concern. "Can I be of some help?"

"No," Emily said. How could anyone be of help, except by murdering Agnes Gelert? Even that would be too late to do any good. Emily's own Adam was a faithless sneak. Nothing could change that. She took out one of the handkerchiefs he had given her for her birthday and blew her nose.

"What's wrong?"

"My husband left me for another woman." On her lips the statement felt like a lie. How could it be true? Her Adam?

"You poor dear," the woman said, patting her back some more. "I know too well how painful that is."

"Do you?"

"It's been fifteen years since my daughter and I were left alone, and I still feel it. But it gets easier to bear with time. And look at it this way: you're young; you can start a whole new life now."

"He took all of our money and lost it."

"Then you will owe him nothing. Do you have children?"

"No children. I don't know why. They simply never came." Why was Emily telling these intimate things to a perfectly strange woman?

"Children are a comfort, but they're a terrible responsibility, too, when you're alone. You'll be fine," the woman said. "You'll start to feel better soon, and then better and better, until you find that you have a happy life again. But I'll give you a valuable piece of advice. You must let him go. People part for a reason, and it's a mistake to try to breathe life into that which is truly dead." She gave Emily a bracing grip on the shoulder and went out, supporting herself on the stick.

Truly dead? How could this be? Emily blew her nose again and composed herself for a dignified exit from the Weatherford. Keeping her chin up, keeping her hat high, she walked out the front door to find that the sun had come out and moisture was rising in steam from the wooden sidewalks of Flagstaff. The mountains stood sharp against the sky, no longer obscured in rain and clouds.

Across the street from the railroad station was a hotel called the Commercial Exchange. It looked more reasonably priced than the Weatherford. Emily turned her steps in that direction, ignoring the rude glances of passing cowboys.

Handbills and posters covered a board fence. *Captain Jinks of the Horse Marines,* in town for two nights only! A creaky old show; in the summer of 1905, Emily had played Madame Aurelia Trentoni, a part that required her to wear a bustle, at the Bangor Opera House. She felt in her purse; a dollar and fifty-seven cents. The big challenge now would be finding the money to get back east.

The Commercial Exchange was much more modest than the Weatherford. To be on the safe side Emily inquired after Adam at the desk; perhaps Howie Kazanow had been lying; but the snotty little clerk assured her that no one by the name of Adam Weiss had ever been registered there.

"Then I'd like a single room, please," she told him. "With a bath."

"Ain't got no single rooms."

"What have you got?"

"You can bunk with some actresses for fifty cents a night. There's a bath down the hall."

Rooming with actresses again. With a sharp sense of déjà vu Emily signed the hotel register "Emily Daggett," her name in the days when she herself was a touring actress. As Emily Daggett she could hide out until she somehow raised train fare to take her back east; in the unlikely event that Adam came looking for her, he would recognize her maiden name. The Commercial Exchange was clearly the place for theater people to stay, right across the street from the railroad tracks, the better to leave town in a hurry.

No one was in the room, up two creaky wooden flights of stairs and down a dirty hallway, when Emily let herself in, although it took her a moment to determine this. Frilly underwear was hung up to dry from a network of improvised wash lines, obscuring her view. The odor of Cashmere Bouquet hand soap rolled out the door in a damp cloud. Wash day. How well she remembered it. She pushed her way through a pair of lacy combinations, stretched out on the nearest bed, and fell into a deep sleep, shoes and all.

When she awoke, three actresses were staring down at her.

"Wake up, sweetie," the little plump one said. "I don't care what that poisonous toad of a clerk told you, you get the daybed. This here bed is mine and Wanda's." She tossed her yellow curls and pointed to the redhead.

"Yeah. Mine and Etta's." Wanda's voice, deep and adenoidal, was flavored with the accents of Cliffside Park, New Jersey.

"I'm so sorry," Emily said. "Of course. I didn't realize."

"Just so there's no mistake." The redhead pointed to a narrow cot under the window. "And that one belongs to Gertrude." That would be the brunette.

"Say, where's your luggage?" Etta said. "Or ain't you got any? We're respectable girls here. Just so there's no mistake about that either."

"My bags are at the station," Emily said. "I'm Emily . . . er . . . Daggett. How do you do."

"Lardy-dah. Her bags are at the station."

"Aw, lay off her, Etta," Wanda said. "Can't you see her clothes? She's a rich lady."

Emily sat up and took her feet off the coverlet. Etta turned her back to her and began feeling the underwear draped over their heads, testing for dryness. She took down a pair of stockings and rolled them up together. "What's a rich lady doing in this dump?"

"There's no need for you all to be so disagreeable. As it happens I'm between engagements."

All three spoke together: "She's an actress!"

The brunette—Gertrude—touched the material in Emily's sleeve. "So where did you get the tailored traveling suit? And that hat?" It was on the nightstand, together with her dye-stained gloves.

"I got them in happier times."

"Oh." The actresses exchanged a look. Happier times meant men with money.

"For a little while I had a rich husband," Emily explained further, not wanting to be mistaken for a chorus trollop. But where, after all, was the shame in that? Here she was with a little over a dollar left in her pocket, no man, no job, and no train fare home, wherever that might be. Chorus trollop would be a step up. It was almost as though the last few years had never happened, as though the brilliant success of Melpomene Moving Pictures had all been a dream, as though Adam himself, with his beautiful face, his handsome shoulders, his money, and his improvidence, had been a dream as well.

"Will it cheer you up to learn that we're leaving tomorrow? You'll have the room all to yourself then," Gertrude said.

"At least until Poison downstairs rents it to someone else," Wanda said. "Better hope it ain't a bunch of cowboys."

"Are there many cowboys in Flagstaff?"

"You'd think so if you was on the stage with us last night."

"You're in *Jinks*, aren't you?" Emily said. "Which one of you is Madame Trentoni?"

"Madame Trentoni and her mother are in the good hotel, lardy-dah," Etta said.

Wanda struck an attitude. "We're the ballet ladies."

Something about her reminded Emily of a vaudeville act she once saw. "Say, aren't you Baby Wanda Rose?"

"Not anymore, honey."

"Young Etta, here, is Hochspitz, the German dancer," Gertrude said. "It's sort of a good part. She gets to do the accent, anyway. So you know the show?"

"I was in it years ago in Bangor, Maine. Why did they put Trentoni in another hotel?"

"Her mother insisted."

Wanda stuck her nose in the air. "Mrs. Swaine wouldn't

let her precious weshious stay in no low-class hotel with the likes of us."

"We're perfectly respectable girls, actually," Gertrude said. "When you get to know us." She squinted into the mirror and touched up her mascara. "Of course Babette de Long's mother doesn't really know us. The dear little thing just joined the troupe a few days ago, after Eunice ran away with the silver baron in Wallace, Idaho."

"Yeah. Can you beat that?" Wanda could scarcely contain her astonishment, or perhaps it was envy. "Married him, too. She's now Mrs. J. J. Bohnert."

"Really. I guess it's lucky you were able to get a replacement on such short notice," Emily said.

"Depends on what you mean by lucky," Etta said. "Ethel Barrymore she ain't. Even if she was a real actress she needs another two weeks in rehearsal."

"Where did they find this woman?"

"I wouldn't even call her a woman," Gertrude said. "They say her mother faked her papers so she can work."

"Dear me."

"She's a movie actress from the West Coast."

"Babette de Long," Emily said. "I think I've heard of her. Her movies are quite popular in New Jersey."

"Wish I was in the movies," Wanda said.

"They say there's money in it," Etta said.

"I used to think so." There had been money, before Adam took it into his head to lose it all. Emily shrugged, thinking, I will be philosophical. "You say Babette de Long isn't old enough to work?"

"Not on the stage. Movies might be another story," Gertrude said.

"Lord save us from stage mothers," Wanda said.

"Well, ladies, if they fire her before the curtain goes up tonight remember I'm at liberty," Emily said. "I know all of Trentoni's lines."

"I know all of Trentoni's lines, too," Gertrude said. "I'm waiting for Sklumpy to figure out that de Long is no good."

"Sklumpy?"

"Mr. Sklump is our producer. De Long's mother, Mrs. Swaine, has some strange power over him." Gertrude took down a few of the frillies and folded them away in a suitcase.

"Not so strange. I could tell you what it is. Hey, that's mine." Wanda seized a petticoat from Gertrude's pile of laundry.

Gertrude looked sidelong at the item, shook her head, and shrugged. "So, Emily, you're an actress. Did you have a stage mother when you were starting out in the business?"

"No. I ran away from home," Emily said. "The circus came to town, and there was a boy on the flying trapeze with beautiful arms."

Wanda eyed her handmade shoes. "You seem to have done pretty well with the circus."

"The circus didn't pan out, really, and neither did Ricky. We parted by mutual agreement in New York City. I got a job right away."

"Lucky you."

"Lucky me. Up to now, anyway."

"So you're not doing so hot these days."

"On the contrary, I'm fine. Aside from being abandoned, stranded, and broke, I've never been better."

"Have you eaten? You look a little peaky," Etta said.

"Not since yesterday. Do you know where I can get a nourishing meal in this town for fifty cents?"

"You can get pie and coffee at Joe's down the street for two bits. The pie is pretty substantial." Etta looked as though she ought to know about substantial. Plenty of meat on her bones. "Hey, Gertrude, ain't those my knickers?"

Emily left the girls to squabble over the clean underwear and set off to find Joe's.

THREE

Joe's, as it happened, was right next door to the First National Bank of Flagstaff. Ah. The bank. When Emily left Fort Lee, New Jersey, the Merchants' Bank of Fort Lee had been stuffed to bursting with her money. Perhaps it would be possible somehow through the wonders of modern communication to lay hands on some of that loot before Howie Kazanow could take it all away. Didn't bankers exchange telegrams and talk to each other on the phone? It seemed to Emily that she had heard of something called a wire transfer. But the banks all closed at two o'clock. The time was now three thirty. There were people inside; something was going on in the bank, money-counting, probably. She rattled the doorknob. The door was locked, and no one inside paid her any attention.

Tomorrow morning, perhaps, she could talk to the local banker. If Emily worked fast she might yet save something out of the wreck with a telephone call or a telegraphed letter of credit.

Holbert Bruns stepped out of the door to the bank as Emily stepped into Joe's Lunch. He tipped his bowler hat and inclined his head. "Mrs. Weiss."

"Mr. Bruns."

He followed her into the beanery. She selected a table by the window and planted herself on a spindly chair. Two cowboys at a nearby table stared at her offensively.

"May I join you?" Bruns said.

As the alternative appeared to be to endure the lewd ogling of cowboys, she said, "Please do." He sat down. The cowboys returned their attention to their beans. How useful. Perhaps she could get Bruns to pick up the check, as long as she was using him. Perhaps he could even give her an introduction to the bank manager. "Tell me," she said, "what were you doing in the bank after hours?"

"My job, Mrs. Weiss, my job."

"The missing persons case."

"The very one." A waitress came to the table. "May I buy you some lunch, Mrs. Weiss? The chicken-fried steak here is excellent."

"Thank you. I'd like that." He ordered chicken-fried steak, whatever in the world that was, and the waitress bellowed the order across the counter to a cook in the kitchen beyond. Greasy smells and sizzling noises wafted through the kitchen door.

So Bruns was at work on his missing persons case. "I

suppose you were checking to see whether your missing person had an account in the bank here, and if so whether he had drawn any money out in recent days."

"You were listening very closely when I described how I work."

"Yes. What did you discover?"

"Whatever I discovered is confidential." The waitress brought them bread and a bottle of ketchup. Bruns spread some ketchup on his bread and took a bite.

"Do you suppose they have butter here?" Emily said.

"No, this is the West. Mrs. Weiss, would you like to help me with my missing persons case?"

"Why would I do that?"

"To amuse yourself. And so that I could safely tell you the details of the case you're so curious about. For then you, too, would be sworn to secrecy. And also for a salary. Most people can use more money."

"I'll have to consider it."

"Then tell me this. Do you think your husband would mind very much if you came to the theater with me tonight?"

"Somehow I think he would not."

"Good. There's a performance of *Captain Jinks of the Horse Marines* at the Majestic Theatre at eight o'clock this evening. I'll call for you at seven thirty. Are you staying at the Weatherford?"

"No, the Commercial Exchange."

"Good," he said.

———

Emily had a porter fetch her trunk from the station, in order that she might select an evening gown in which to enjoy the nightlife of Flagstaff. When the trunk arrived the actresses were sitting around in their corsets and petticoats running lines for *Jinks*. Gertrude was reading Trentoni's part, on the slim chance that Babette de Long would drop dead before the evening's performance. She was pretty good.

When Emily opened the trunk and began to rummage among her silks and furs, the actresses cast their scripts aside and crowded around.

"Let us help you unpack," Gertrude offered.

"Yes, do. Look at this, girls." Etta pulled out the purple velvet with the embroidered roses and paillettes. "That's the stuff! Did you ever see anything so fancy?"

"Say, that looks almost my size." Wanda held it up to herself. "You wouldn't want to sell it, would you?"

"I wouldn't mind," Emily said. "I wouldn't mind selling most of these things." At once the actresses fell upon her evening clothes like tigers on the finery of the East Indian boy in the children's fable. Give me your little purple jacket with the gold buttons or I'll eat you up! Give me your little red shoes! Gertrude and Wanda wore more or less the same dress size as Emily except for their corseted waists and more generous endowments in the bosom. Etta, too fat for any of the dresses, swanked about the room in Emily's second-best opera cloak while the other two were squeezing into Emily's frocks.

When the dust of the final transaction had settled, Emily still had all of her undergarments, most of her Paris hats, including the new one, her winter coat, her good traveling suit, one cotton frock, three pairs of shoes, two shirtwaists, and an evening dress that was the last word in Paris. She told herself it was an improvement: she now had a simple wardrobe of tremendous elegance. She also had more money than before. Train fare! At least enough to take her back east as far as Chicago.

The woman in the ladies' lounge had been perfectly right about the way things would start to look better. Clearly Adam never had been the man Emily thought he was. She had loved a hollow shell stuffed with her own hopes and wishes. The real Adam bossed her, bullied her, prospered as a result of her work, took advantage of her good nature, and betrayed her with cheap actresses. Now that his foot was no longer on her neck she was free. Well rid of him. Rejoice!

Emily was moved by this notion to jump up off the daybed and do a clog step. The actresses, still dressed in Emily's fancy gowns, formed a kick line beside her, laughing to kill themselves. Wanda had to hike the black-and-white-striped hobble skirt well up on her thighs in order to kick. Another thing I'm well rid of, Emily thought, a real crippler, that skirt. Adam had liked it. Well, he would, wouldn't he?

"But what will you wear to the Majestic tonight?" Gertrude said.

"This." She held up her evening dress, a divine high-waisted creation of embroidered mauve silk, soft and flattering as a lover's whisper. "It's a Poiret."

"A Pwa-*ray*. Lardy-dah," Etta said.

"You're going to wear that?" Gertrude said. "In Flagstaff, Arizona? The waistline is way up under your bazooms."

"That's so it won't need a corset."

"You may be lynched. Respectable women wear corsets in the West."

"I don't own a corset."

Wanda offered to let her borrow a corset, but Emily refused.

"She's a New Woman," Etta said. "I read about them in *Delineator* magazine."

"Well, good luck, dearie," Gertrude said. "Maybe if you put enough of those ostrich feathers on top of your head no one will notice your shape."

"Now you're getting the idea," Emily said.

But as it happened the ostrich feathers were not enough to take Holbert Bruns's eyes away from Emily's slim figure when he picked her up for the show. A bellhop came up to the room and announced that Mr. Bruns was waiting for Mrs. Weiss in the lobby. The rickety stairs were not the grand staircase of the Waldorf-Astoria; still, by taking the material of her skirt in one hand, placing one foot carefully in front of another, and keeping her chin high, she was able to make a tolerably impressive descent.

"You look lovely," he said.

"Thank you."

A soft desert breeze stirred Emily's ostrich feathers as the two walked to the theater, Emily picking her way along the muddy wooden sidewalk so as not to ruin her satin evening pumps. The Majestic was a short walk from the Commercial Exchange, right next door to the Weatherford.

Emily had never imagined so many cowboys in one place together, hooting, whistling, and smelling of cows. Bruns's tickets were for front-row center seats, close enough to the stage for Emily to notice the smoke of the oil burning in the footlights. Her dancer friends did not appear in the first act. Most of that was taken up with business between the men, where Jinks bet his friend Charlie a thousand dollars that he could get up a flirtation with Madame Trentoni. The cowboys grew restless. They had come here to see good-looking women.

Babette de Long, when she finally made her appearance as Trentoni, tripping down the gangplank in front of a painted canvas ocean liner, drew tremendous applause. She was exquisitely beautiful, with masses of honey-colored hair, extremely young, and barely competent as an actress; her huge blue eyes, only lightly accented with stage makeup, were focused somewhere beyond the back wall of the theater; from time to time her lip trembled, possibly because she kept forgetting her lines. Holbert Bruns seemed completely absorbed in the girl's performance.

"She's very pretty," Emily whispered.

"She's very troubled," Bruns replied. "That girl has a lot on her mind. I'd give a great deal to know exactly what."

"Is she part of your case?"

"If you were to accept a job with me I could tell you."

Late in the first act Babette de Long went up in her lines completely. As she stood frozen in the middle of her scene with Jinks and the policeman, the hiss of the prompter could be heard from the wings: "'Do you take me for an Irish dressmaker with a French name smuggling in her winter models!'" The girl stared around her like a hunted thing, her gaze resting at last on Emily.

"'Do you take me for an Irish dressmaker!'" Emily prompted. Cowboys on either side of her guffawed. Instead of picking up her cue the girl broke down weeping and rushed off the stage.

The curtain closed. A man in formal attire—this must be Maestro Sklump—came out of the place where the tatty curtains met in the middle, the chain bulging out of a rupture in the bottom hem, and announced that due to the sudden illness of Miss de Long, Gertrude Canty would carry on in the part of Trentoni. The audience greeted this announcement with boos and vegetables, but when the curtain opened again, revealing Gertrude in de Long's dress, even tighter on her than it had been on de Long, they began once again to cheer, whistle, and hoot. The cowboys appreciated a good corset and bustle, never mind how far out of fashion it was.

Bruns tugged at Emily's arm. "Come with me. I'm going backstage to see if I can talk to Miss de Long."

"Must we? I'd like to see how Gertrude does."

"Gertrude will do fine. Come on. Maybe Miss de Long's mother will let a woman get in to talk to her. See if you can find out what's the matter with her."

They ignored the grumbling of the cowboys whose boots they were stepping on in the dark and made for the stage right fire exit. One of the cowboys pinched Emily's uncorseted bottom; when she yelped the other cowboys shushed her. Backstage, a low murmur came from the dressing room with the star on the door. Slowly it opened. A man with a doctor's bag came out frowning and shaking his head.

Bruns gave Emily a poke in the ribs. She stepped forward and said, "Excuse me, may I speak to Miss de Long?" Over the doctor's shoulder she saw Babette de Long stretched out on a fainting couch in her underthings, still in her makeup, her eyes closed, her honey-colored hair spread out all over the headrest. A woman in evening clothes bent over her, stroking her forehead and murmuring. The woman's face was hidden, but there was something—

Two toughs stepped forward and blocked the doorway, employees of the theater. Well, of course they would have people to keep the cowboys away from their little star. "Miss de Long ain't seeing anyone," they said, and slammed the door in Emily's face.

Emily turned to Holbert Bruns and shrugged. "Nothing doing, as you can see. Can I go back and see the show now?"

"You want to step on those cowboys again?"

"No."

"Then let's go to the Weatherford and have some supper."

So they did, chicken-fried steak again, with turnips this time and apple pie for dessert. Hardly anybody stared at Emily's Poiret and ostrich feathers. One of those who did was the detestable Howie Kazanow, dining in the corner with a handful of his coarse cronies. It was nothing personal, since he didn't know who she was, for which she was thankful.

Still, if he made another of his insulting remarks Emily would be bound in honor to go over and confront him, probably with violence. She fantasized about picking up the bottle of wine that Holbert Bruns had ordered and pouring the contents over Kazanow's head. Then she thought, No, a smart crack across the face with the bottle. She imagined the sound of his cheekbone breaking. She imagined the sound of Adam's cheekbone breaking. Bruns kept watching the front door, waiting for the return of Miss de Long.

As they were finishing their pie a bellhop came into the dining room bearing a silver tray with a yellow envelope on it. "Telegram for Mrs. Weiss!" he sang. "Tele-gray-am for Mrs. Adam Weiss!"

"Over here, son," Bruns called, before Emily could stop him. He tipped the boy and handed her the telegram, smiling, like a Great Dane happily offering some inexpressibly nasty thing to its mistress. She tore it open, neglecting to thank him, ignoring the gloating sneer of Howie Kazanow, who now knew she was Adam's abandoned wife, the chorus trollop, already dining in a hotel with another man. The telegram was from Adam. He was in Mexico.

AGNES GELERT AND I DEEPLY IN LOVE STOP OBTAINING MEXICAN DIVORCE SO WE CAN BE MARRIED STOP FORGET ME STOP IM NOT WORTHY OF YOU STOP ADAM

Deeply in love? Where had she heard that phrase before? Wait a minute. Didn't you have to have some sort of personal depth, before you could be deeply in love? The pie in her mouth was like ashes and glue. She swallowed it with difficulty. Never again would she look at apple pie without a horrible feeling in her stomach.

"What is it, Mrs. Weiss? Are you all right? Your lips are turning blue."

She handed the missive to Bruns. He read it over and said, "He got the last part right anyway."

"Thank you."

"Mrs. Weiss, I don't want to say I told you so—"

"Then don't."

"Right." He took out his pipe and filled it. "Nevertheless, I'm still here if you want me. In any capacity."

"So I see."

"What are you going to do now?"

"I don't know." In her thirty years of life she had never been so angry.

"You'll need money," Bruns said.

Money. Yes. "I was planning to see the manager of the local bank in the morning about transferring some money out of my account in Fort Lee so that I can go back east. Failing that, maybe I can get work with the touring company of *Jinks*. They're short a dancer, what with one thing and another."

"Come to Hollywood with me."

She blinked. Here it was, the first step on the road to ruin. "I'm not a common chorus trollop, Mr. Bruns."

Bruns blushed to the roots of his hair. "Oh, dear, no, of course not. Please don't misunderstand my offer. I need a business associate, a woman. I need *you*. You're not a common anything. I know that."

"Then I appreciate the offer, Mr. Bruns. But the truth is, I'm not a detective either." In the corner, Kazanow was smirking. Just let him say one thing. Her hand crept toward the wine bottle.

Emily encountered Kazanow's smirk again first thing in the morning when she was going into the First National Bank of Flagstaff, smart in her traveling suit, as he was coming out, flashy in his spats and big gold watch chain. He tipped his straw hat; she cut him dead. They had not, after all, been properly introduced.

In the bank manager's office a lingering smell of cigar smoke whispered of the recent presence of Kazanow. "It's no good asking for a wire transfer of money from Fort Lee, Mrs. Weiss. That isn't your money anymore."

"Well, if you're willing to accept the word of a snake like Howard Kazanow—"

"Ma'am, I was sitting there at the poker table when Mr. Kazanow won all your husband's money."

"Oh."

"I'm afraid there's nothing I can do to help you. Of course, if you're interested in a position, I am in need of a housekeeper." His smile suggested that a variety of duties might be involved, each more distasteful to Emily than the last.

"No, thank you," she said. "Kind of you to offer, but I'm afraid being a housekeeper is not in my line."

———

She went back to the hotel. The *Jinks* girls were gone, bag and baggage. Thinking to catch up with them before the troupe left town, she threw her few things in a suitcase and ran for the train, leaving her trunk standing empty.

Clouds of black coal smoke drifted over the roof of the passenger station. The chuff and grind of the locomotive met her ear; the sight of the passenger cars of the California Limited met her eye, accelerating, zipping past her now, click-clack, click-clack. She could see faces in the windows. Her actress friends from *Jinks*. Babette de Long and a veiled woman who must have been de Long's dragon of a mother. Howie Kazanow. Kazanow's friend, the salesman, traveling in ladies' underwear or whatever it was he sold. Everybody was going west. No one was left in Flagstaff but Emily and a lot of heartless strangers.

FOUR

And yet, among the Indians, cowboys, bankers, sheep farmers' wives, urchins, grocer's boys, and saloon keepers who bustled about the streets of Flagstaff when Emily finally dried her eyes and came out of the ladies' room of the train station, one familiar face shone forth. Unlike the rest of known humanity, Holbert Bruns had not left town on the California Limited.

He tipped his hat and smiled. For an instant Emily thought of asking for his professional services as a detective. About three o'clock that morning, as she tossed and turned on the rock pile of a daybed in the actresses' hotel room, it had occurred to her that the telegram that was delivered to her at the Weatherford, purporting to be from Adam, might be a fake. For one thing she had never heard her husband use the phrase "deeply in love." But it was the sort of thing that fell from Agnes Gelert's lips every time she met something new in pants.

Emily had tried and tried to visualize the Adam she knew composing that telegram, perhaps dictating it to a telegraph operator in Ciudad Juárez. The thing was impossible. Several alternatives presented themselves to her sleepless mind. All of them ended painfully with Adam and Miss Gelert falling into bed (except the one where Adam was tortured to death by Zapatistas, whereupon the Zapatistas faked the telegram and buried him under a cactus). The most likely scenario was that Adam had delegated the composition of the telegram to Agnes. It was more her style, and more his way of doing things. "Send my wife a telegram, darling. Tell her something that will settle her mind." The words of the desk clerk at the Weatherford, ignored when she first heard them, now rang in Emily's ears, saying someone had been living at the hotel with Adam as his wife. Something was going on. But, deeply in love?

Here was an idea. Perhaps Agnes had gotten tired of Adam, murdered him, buried him under a cactus, and faked the telegram so that no one would come looking for him.

Holbert Bruns's manner was jarringly cheerful. "Good morning, Mrs. Weiss. I trust you slept well."

"Your trust is misplaced. I did not sleep well. And I wish to be called Miss Daggett."

"Good morning, Miss Daggett, then. How did things go with the bank?"

"Not well."

"Let me buy you breakfast."

"I'm not sure I should."

"Let your new employer buy you breakfast. We can expense it. The client pays."

Was her back to the wall now? Was there no other recourse but to go to work for the completely untrustworthy Holbert Bruns? He held the door to Joe's open for her, and they went in.

"Suppose I were to take you up on your offer," she said. "What would your business associate be expected to do?"

"Well, now, as I told you before, I'm working on a disappearance. A man has disappeared; my client would like to know what became of him. A woman can go places I can't go, ask questions I can't ask. Your help would be very valuable."

"It's not the sort of thing I see myself doing as a career."

"Suppose I could get you a job in films."

"Not an acting job," she said. "I don't want to do that anymore."

"Something else, then. Wait. Let me make a call." There was a pay phone at the end of the counter. Bruns put in a person-to-person call to Carl Laemmle in Hollywood, California.

Carl Laemmle, the famous movie mogul! What would Adam think, if Emily went to work for Carl Laemmle? This was a man whose career closely paralleled Adam's own; he had started out in Chicago running nickelodeons; he moved on to distribution; he went into moving picture production in 1909, the same year that Adam did, and for the same reason: to put a finger in the eye of Thomas Edison and his Motion Picture Patents Company. Now known as IMP, Laemmle's Independent Moving Picture Company of America ran a studio in Hollywood out of reach of Edison and the Trust detectives (or so it was hoped). IMP formed a part of the newly organized Universal Film Manufacturing Company, the up-and-coming movie conglomerate. People in the industry said Carl Laemmle was making heaps of money. Adam believed this, and was consumed with envy of the man.

In her mind Emily composed a telegram:

DEAR ADAM STOP I AM CARL LAEMMLE'S WOMAN NOW STOP KINDLY DROP DEAD STOP EMILY

But he probably wouldn't feel the sting of her scorn. He was a prisoner of the hypnotic eyes of Agnes Gelert. Years would pass before Adam took notice of anything Emily said or did, and by then it would be too late; she herself would no longer care whether she made an impression on him.

Bruns hung up the phone and sat down at the counter to wait for his call to go through.

"Mr. Laemmle is your client?"

"He is."

"And the missing person?"

"Wait."

She waited. The counterman asked what they wanted, and Bruns ordered coffee, scrambled eggs, bacon, and toast for both of them. At last the phone rang.

A brief exchange of pleasantries, and then, "I want to ask you to put a woman I know on your payroll, Mr. Laemmle.

Er . . . Miss Emily Daggett. She'll be useful to me as an assistant. She has intelligence and nerve." Laemmle said something. Bruns beckoned Emily to the phone.

The mogul's voice buzzed out of the earpiece: "Miss Daggett? Carl Laemmle here. Mr. Bruns tells me you are a competent detective."

"I am not a detective. I can't think what gave Mr. Bruns such an idea."

"You won't work for IMP as a detective?"

"That's not the sort of work I want to do."

"What do you want to do?"

"I want to direct moving pictures." The answer fell out of her mouth without thought. She was a little surprised, but there it was. She wanted to direct moving pictures.

"Really," the mogul said. "Do you have any experience along these lines?"

"Yes. I directed *Lynching at Laramie* and *Silly Sally* for Melpomene. Enormously successful one-reelers."

"Good. I'll hire you to direct a moving picture. While you're doing that you can find out what happened to Ross McHenry."

"Of course I'll want a contract," Emily said. Ross McHenry? Was he missing? IMP's biggest male star? But weren't they in the middle of filming a feature-length—

"I'll have my lawyers draw up a contract right away," Laemmle said. "How soon can you get to Hollywood?"

Some movie director's idea of a liveried chauffeur met them at the railway station in Los Angeles, booted and gauntleted, wearing smart jodhpurs. He threw their bags in the back of the studio's Cadillac Model 30 limousine. Emily was startled to see that he wore a diamond in his right earlobe. Los Angeles was certainly a different world.

She took a deep breath before getting in the car. A different world! Sunshine and palm trees. The air was nothing like the air in New Jersey. You could smell orange groves even in the city, even over the coal smoke and horse dung and the smell of cars. Wouldn't Adam love it here? It wouldn't have surprised her to see camels.

As the chauffeur jumped into the driver's seat Holbert Bruns leaned over the back and said, "Nice car."

"Yeah," the chauffeur said.

"You don't have to crank it, I see."

"No," the chauffeur said. "Brand-new Cadillac, everything electric. Electric starter. Electric horn." He sounded the horn, which went "a-*oo*gah!" and caused an old lady walking in front of the limousine to jump a foot in the air.

"It's one of those new Klaxons, isn't it?" Bruns said. "I understand those were invented in the Edison laboratories."

"We don't talk about Edison here in Los Angeles," the chauffeur said.

"Why not? Isn't the federal government closing down the Motion Picture Patents Company?"

"Maybe. Maybe not. Just the same we don't talk about Edison. A lot of people came out here to get away from him."

"Here I thought it was for the climate."

"That, too."

The chauffeur put his wonderful car in gear and bulled

his way into the midst of traffic, sounding his horn some more. Emily clung to the strap with one hand and clutched her hat with the other. She wasn't the only one uneasy with this man's driving style; Holbert Bruns's knuckles showed white where he gripped the seat in front of him. "Say, don't I know you?" Bruns said.

"Don't think so, boss."

"Yes, I do. You're Chicago Eddie Green."

"I ain't been Chicago Eddie Green since I came out west. Now I'm just Eddie Green."

"How long have you been in Los Angeles, Eddie?"

Teeth glinted in the rearview mirror, almost outshining the diamond in Eddie's ear. What a smile. "Long enough to forget about Chicago. Los Angeles is the greatest city in the world, boss." A car swooped toward them. He wrenched the steering wheel, throwing Emily into Bruns's lap.

Politely he helped her right herself, remarking, "I hear that Los Angeles has the highest per capita rate of death by auto in the civilized world."

"We got everything here," Eddie said. "Sunshine, orange trees . . . wait till we get to Hollywood." A-*oo*gah! The Cadillac took another wild leap and paused at an intersection to let three streetcars go by.

The very highest? Emily couldn't believe it. "Worse than New York?"

"New York is fourth," Bruns said. "But the report was on deaths by auto, not deaths by fright."

The chauffeur turned to look at Bruns, narrowly missing two pedestrians. "You complaining about the way I drive? Because I ain't had any complaints up to now."

Manly tempers were about to collide. Emily changed the subject: "Can you tell me what that white building is?"

"Yeah, that's the Masonic Temple. Greatest city in the world. Greatest public transportation system, too. You can get anywhere you want to on the Red Car. Over there is the tallest building in town." He carried on a running travelogue as he dodged and darted northward. Eventually the traffic thinned, the tall buildings fell behind them, the asphalt roads became packed clay, and the wooded hills rose up in their faces.

"This is Hollywood, folks," Eddie Green said. He pulled up and parked in front of a low cinder block building with a glass-roofed barnlike structure behind it. Paint was flaking off the arched wooden sign surmounting the doorway: IMP MOTION PICTURES. "And this here's Mr. Laemmle's studio. Come on in and I'll show you around."

"I've seen it, thanks," Holbert Bruns said.

"Perhaps the lady then." Did he just wink at her? "You can leave your bags in the car. I'll take care of 'em." He held the front door open with an elegant gesture, and Emily swept into the hot, dry vestibule, followed by Bruns. "That's Mr. Laemmle's office there." Through the glass door was a reception area, rows of chairs under the eye of a gum-chewing blonde behind a desk. The blonde looked up at Eddie and stuck out her tongue. She wore enough makeup around her eyes to be going on the stage.

"That's Millie. She's a good kid. Down that hall"—he

gestured to the left—"are the ladies' facilities, in case you need the ladies' facilities, and then the dressing rooms and the studio where they shoot the films. C'mon, I'll show you." At the far end of the hall he opened the door onto the studio, its stages the scene of frantic activity. Emily stared at King Baggot, making movie love to Miriam Aiken before the cameras to the sound of hammers, saws, a bellowing director, and a string quartet.

"They're filming three pictures in there right now," Eddie said. He shut the door and pointed to another: "That door goes to the back lot. This door here is Mr. Laemmle's conference room. Over there the processing rooms. Down that way"—he gestured to the right—"is wardrobe, and at the end of the hall the commissary. Very important, the commissary, in case you get hungry. The food is cheap and not half bad. Outside and around the corner are the garages. That's where you'll find me." Yes, he did wink. He distinctly winked.

"So. Welcome to IMP. Go see Mr. Laemmle right away. He's expecting youse."

The Great Man sat waiting for them behind a cluttered desk in his office, which office reeked of cigars and women's perfume, no doubt the effluvia of a parade of real and would-be actresses. Framed movie stills decorated the walls, as well as head shots of the stars: Miriam Aiken, King Baggot, Florence Lawrence, Marilyn Slater, Ross McHenry.

Mr. Laemmle beamed at Emily and Bruns when they came in. He stood up and gave Emily his soft little paw to shake. She was bemused to find that the biggest mogul in independent pictures was shorter than she was, starting to go bald, and that there were freckles on the top of his head.

He spoke with a Middle European accent. "So you want to direct pictures, Miss Daggett." He sat down again and gestured toward the two other chairs in the room. Emily glanced at Bruns. When he sat in one of the chairs she sat in the other.

"Yes," she said.

"I'm surprised. I would have thought a woman with your looks would sooner be in front of a camera."

"Acting gets old. I don't want to do that anymore."

Mr. Laemmle thumbed through a pile of papers, then consulted a calendar, humming softly all the while. At length he looked up. "I think maybe you can direct *Captain Jinks of the Horse Marines*. We're going to make a feature-length film out of it. You know the show?"

"Intimately."

"Good. It's a woman's picture, right? Perfect for you. And for our own Babette de Long."

Oh, no. Not her. "When do you want to begin shooting?"

"As soon as possible. But we'll talk about that later. First we have to finish *Dark Star of India*. Find Ross McHenry. We're shooting around him, but if he doesn't show up in the next five days IMP stands to lose a million dollars. He left the studio three weeks ago Friday at five o'clock. Hasn't been seen since."

"I can show you a picture of him, Miss Daggett," Holbert Bruns said, reaching into an inner pocket of his coat.

"No need," Emily said. "Every woman in America has

that face engraved on her heart." And not only the face. She remembered vividly his performance in *Revenge of the Pirate Captain,* the feature-length movie Adam took her to see at the Lyceum in New York City the day before he left Fort Lee. What a picture. What a stunning-looking man McHenry was. It would be good to find him, to see him in the flesh. Maybe even with his shirt off.

"Right," Mr. Laemmle said. "Every woman in America. And also in Europe. That's the problem. We have to have his face to sell this picture."

"Maybe he ran off to Mexico with a chorus trollop," Emily said. The men looked at her strangely. "I mean, doesn't everybody? From time to time."

"No," Holbert Bruns said. "Very few men do that, in fact, Miss Daggett. Hardly any in the middle of a success-ful career."

Carl Laemmle cleared his throat. "Ross McHenry is a deeply spiritual fellow, or so he always told us. He doesn't even eat meat. Also none of our chorus trollops are missing."

"The studio does a head count every morning," Bruns explained. Emily thought, Why am I doing this? I'm not a detective. It's going to be a lot of trouble. I should chuck this whole business and go get a job as a waitress. There are plenty of restaurants on Sunset Boulevard, I saw them when we were driving by. I would be my own woman and not have to jump around at the beck and call of moguls. Working for Holbert Bruns, who never tells me anything. She saw herself slinging hash at the grateful hungry of Hollywood. Then she imagined Adam coming back from

Mexico with that horrible woman on his arm, strolling into the restaurant, forcing her to wait on him, stiffing her on the tip.

"Is there anything else you need, Miss Daggett? You can see the paymaster for an advance against your salary."

The paymaster. Good. But—"What about Babette de Long? I mean, what does she . . . ?"

"Little Babs," Carl Laemmle said dreamily. "I'm happy to say that she will be your Trentoni for *Captain Jinks*."

"Will she, now."

"She is quite close to Mr. McHenry, I understand. Like a daughter to him."

"Perhaps I should ask her about him," Emily said.

"Good idea. Only watch out for the mother. The woman is difficult."

A studio flunky stuck his head in the door. "Smithson is ready for you now, Uncle Carl," he said.

"I'm going to have to go and do this other thing," Mr. Laemmle said. "Take these files and study them." He held out a brown accordionfold envelope with a string tied around it.

"Is this the scenario for *Captain Jinks*?"

"No, it's the files on Mr. McHenry and some of the other people working on the picture. It may be that you'll find it helpful." He stood up, came around the desk, and shook her hand again. "We've reserved a room for you at the Hotel Hollywood, Miss Daggett, where Mr. Bruns is staying. I want to hear from both of you tomorrow, and every morning after that until you find him. The sooner

53

we can track down Ross McHenry and finish shooting *Dark Star of India* the sooner you can get on with *Captain Jinks*."

It seemed like a simple matter. Yet, perhaps not. Recalling Holbert Bruns's description of his methods and expectations in the matter of missing persons, Emily found herself considering the question of foul play.

FIVE

The Hotel Hollywood was the sort of down-at-the-heels resort
that Emily had become used to in the early days at Fort
Lee, when they had to rent dressing rooms, before Melpomene built their own studio and stopped filming every
picture in the open air. It wasn't cold, the way the Potts
Hotel had been; this was Southern California, after all,
and there were palm trees growing in the yard; but her
bathwater ran out of the faucet in a tepid brown trickle,
the ashtray next to the bed was smudged and smelly, and
the thin cotton mattress where she laid out her summer
dress gave off whiffs of mold.

And yet, unlike the Potts establishment, the Hollywood
was not a haunt of beautiful young movie people. Out-
doors on the veranda, nearly all the rocking chairs were

occupied by ancient crones and geezers. These might have been the very founders of California, exhausted from their long labors, perhaps disappointed in the results, staring unblinkingly at the view from the veranda: the wooded hills, a few half-built houses, an orange grove, the oiled dirt road in front of the hotel, the occasional automobile or horse-drawn wagon. When Emily passed in front of them to join Holbert Bruns, who was holding the last rocker for her, the old people paid her no more attention than would a row of lizards.

Emily settled into the rocker. "What do you want me to do for the rest of today?"

"Have a good supper and get some sleep." He patted her knee.

Strange electrical jolts traveled up and down her spine, but she ignored them and said, "What are you going to do?" as if nothing were happening.

"I'm going into Los Angeles and cruise the gin joints, gambling hells, opium dens, bawdy houses, and lairs of perversion, looking for Ross McHenry. Now, I know you're a sophisticated woman, Miss Daggett, but I don't think you want to come along for this."

"No. No, I don't. You're quite right." Was she being cowardly? Wouldn't a real detective pull herself together and go visit the lairs of perversion?

"In case I don't find him, and I probably won't, him being such a spiritual fellow and all, your job will be to go up to Krotona first thing tomorrow morning and talk to his neighbors. You want to be well rested for this. You're going to pose as a seeker."

"A seeker."

"Nothing to it. You behave as if you have no idea what's real, spout words like simulism and reptilianism, and talk about your astral body."

"How will I find Krotona?"

Holbert Bruns reached out his hand in the direction of the Hollywood Hills, spreading his fingers. His hand was attractive, square but not stubby, strong but not brutal. Adam's hands, Emily recalled, were almost effeminate in the way his fingers tapered. She shifted her gaze to the hills.

"Up there," Bruns said. "Do you know anything about Theosophy?"

"It's something like Christian Science, isn't it?"

"Something like that, yes, and something like New Thought, and it was founded by some dame in Russia, who's dead now. Anyhow the Theosophical Society has built a large compound up in those hills, just east of Vine Street. They call the compound Krotona. You can get there by streetcar. Ross McHenry has a bungalow on Temple Hill Drive." Out came the pipe; Bruns filled it with tobacco, tamped it with his pinky, and lit it, puffing.

"Is he one of the Theosophicals, or whatever they call themselves?"

"That's one of the things I'd like to know about him. He keeps his private life very private, which is hard to do when every woman in America wants to know everything there is to know."

"His publicity folder is good and fat. There must be—"

"I think you'll find that nothing real about Ross McHenry is in his publicity folder. But read it anyway. For one thing, it's very important to our employer for the moviegoing public to continue to believe it's all true. When you're finished you might type up a brief report of the salient points, just a paragraph or so. I had the hotel staff provide you with a typewriter and some paper."

"What do you know about him, other than what's in the file?"

"Nothing. I've never met him. Everybody I've talked to has a different story about the sort of man Ross McHenry is. I talked to a fisherman who claimed he saw him passed out in a waterfront tavern in San Pedro. Some sailors came and shanghaied him on board a slow boat to China, he said. Then there was a Paiute Indian who claimed he went hunting with him in Truckee and saw him get eaten by a bear."

"So did Ross McHenry drink, then? Or did he ever go hunting?"

"Beats me. It depends on who you ask. If he's one of the Theosophists, he's supposed to be a teetotaling vegetarian."

"Tell me what you found out in the bank in Flagstaff, and what Little Babs has to do with the case."

"You want the facts?"

"I want the gossip."

"It might not be any more true than the Billie Burke story."

"The Billie Burke story was completely true, as I'm sure you know quite well." If only she hadn't interfered with Agnes Gelert's plans, Emily thought. If only. That woman would be in Europe by now with Billie Burke's husband, instead of in Mexico with Emily's.

Bruns gave her a sharp look. "You're grinding your teeth, Miss Daggett."

"Am I?"

"Try to keep your mind on the case. The gossip goes like this. McHenry had all his money transferred to the bank in Flagstaff, where he was going to meet Little Babs and run away with her, to the chagrin and distress of her mother, the ogre."

"And?"

There was no trace of his money ever having been in the bank there, and no sign of his ever having been in Flagstaff. Or in Coronado Junction, or Chicago, or any of the other places he was said to have run off to."

"But, Babs—"

"Was rumored to be wildly in love with him, but again it's studio gossip. That's why I need a woman on this case. As odd as it may seem to you, there are people who don't trust me well enough to tell me certain things."

"I can't imagine it," she said.

The sun sank slowly behind a line of trees; the old lizards stirred expectantly in their rockers. The end of another day.

And the beginning of another night without Adam in her bed. Emily wondered what her husband and that miserable woman were doing right now. Drinking tequila, probably, dancing the tango, or the cucaracha, or whatever it was people danced south of the border, or maybe sitting holding hands while they watched the sun sink behind the mountains of the Sierra Nevada. A tear found its way out of her eye and ran down her cheek.

"Now, now, Miss Daggett, none of that," Holbert Bruns said in a soft little moo. He produced a clean linen handkerchief and, reaching over, blotted up the tear. "Things will look better tomorrow."

"People keep telling me that."

"They tell you that because it's true. In the meantime I need you to concentrate on your work. We have a missing actor to find."

A gong sounded, the dinner gong, Emily guessed, by the way the lizards all came creaking to their feet and began to shuffle toward the dining room.

"How is the food here?" she said.

"Pretty bad. I'm going to forgo the pleasure of it this evening. Instead I'm going back to the city now and look for McHenry in all the joints. Eat your supper as best you can, read those files, do a little typing, get some sleep. You'll need your strength tomorrow. I'll see you at breakfast."

Ross McHenry's publicity file bulged with pictures of the man, eight-by-ten head shots, movie stills, five-by-eight glossies for distribution to the big-city dailies along with typed puff pieces headed FOR IMMEDIATE RELEASE. His eyes were sparkling and compelling, even without makeup; his body was that of a circus acrobat. Not very different from Ricky's.

Emily took a sip of her hot milk, pulled the covers up around her armpits, and began to write down in her notebook the things she read in the files.

McHenry was born in Shanghai in 1885 to Christian missionary parents, said the publicity release. Orphaned in the Boxer Rebellion, he worked his way back to the States as a deckhand on a tramp steamer. For years he earned his bread as a longshoreman and a short-order cook, until the happy day when he turned up in Hollywood to work in pictures, making his great gift available to movie-goers everywhere.

Bushwah, Emily thought. All of it. If that man wasn't a circus performer Emily was prepared to eat the entire publicity folder, with or without ketchup. He wasn't any twenty-eight years old either. Look at those creases in his forehead, look at those bags under his eyes.

Here was a blown-up snapshot of the cast and crew of *Dark Star of India*. The photograph was a good illustration of the principle that the outward appearance of a movie actor had to be unusually vivid. Even though no one was in makeup, all the actors in the shot drew the eye, beautiful or at least interesting in their forms and faces, and all the nonactors in the picture, cameramen, and so forth, seemed faded and colorless. But who was that in the background, gleaming like another star? Carl Laemmle's chauffeur, Chicago Eddie Green, lurking in the doorway with his hands folded together over his flat belly, staring at McHenry with hooded eyes and an oily smile.

Strange. Perhaps he coveted McHenry's part in the movie.

And here was McHenry's most famous studio portrait, the one in the black hat where his hair was slightly too long and curly for the fashion. Emily propped it up on the night table and took a good look at it. She decided he had a weak lower lip. Almost certainly he had decamped to Mexico with a chorus trollop, perhaps one from some other studio, since the ones at IMP were all accounted for. Tomorrow she would advance this theory with more force. Perhaps Holbert Bruns would send some other operative down there to look for him, someone who might incidentally check up on Adam.

The rest of McHenry's file consisted of clippings from newspapers, some of them stories copied verbatim from the press releases sent out by the studio. Now, here was an interesting thing, a sheaf of gossip columns marked *Los Angeles Examiner* with various dates, under the byline of Hester Mink.

Unnamed sources had observed Mr. McHenry dining at this hot spot or that with this or that young movie actress, according to Miss Mink, the actress always coincidentally under contract to the IMP Studios. The most recent column suggested that McHenry and his current costar, Marilyn Slater, were involved in a flaming romance. "*Dark Star of India* promises to be a scorcher," Miss Mink wrote. Probably studio propaganda, but worth checking. Emily turned to the file on Marilyn Slater.

Another collection of charming lies put together by Mr. Laemmle's publicity people. Had Miss Slater really grown up on a cotton plantation in Louisiana? Discovered the tomb of an Egyptian pharaoh? Swum the English Channel? Rejected marriage proposals from the crowned heads of Europe? Halfway through these fictions Emily's eyelids began to droop. Enough for one night. She put all the files back in the envelope. In the morning she would deal with the typing.

On a sudden impulse she pried the picture of Adam out of her grandmother's silver locket, put it in the bedside ashtray, and set fire to it with the hotel matches. Such a tiny flame. She dropped off to sleep with the smoke of burnt Adam still in her nose.

When Emily awoke, the California sun was streaming in the open window along with birdsong and a smell of orange blossoms. She put on her robe and slippers and pattered down the linoleum hallway to the bathroom. For the first morning since reading her husband's fatal telegram she didn't feel sick to her stomach. Twenty days had passed since her last sight of the man. She was getting over him. But why should she take the trouble to get over him? He couldn't have seriously left her, it was a bad joke, it was a hoax of some sort.

She washed, dressed, pecked a few lines about Ross McHenry, and scribbled off a note to Adam in care of general delivery, Ciudad Juárez, telling him where to find her when he recovered his senses. Then she made her way downstairs to the dining room, rather hoping that Holbert Bruns would tell her he had found McHenry passed out in an opium den somewhere in Chinatown. That would be the end of this silly detective business, and the beginning of the next phase of Emily's life, her Hollywood directing career. *Captain Jinks*. So what if it wasn't *War and Peace*? She could take on *War and Peace* later.

Bruns was indeed waiting for her, bleary-eyed over a slice of toast and a cup of coffee. By his smell and appearance she deduced that he had not been to bed.

"What's the news?" she said. "Did you find him?"

"I didn't find him, no, though I talked to some people who saw him some time ago in a Turkish bathhouse on Fourth Street, or so they said." Bruns stared into his coffee cup as if its contents were of tremendous significance. "It's a place where a certain sort of man goes to find other men like himself." He stirred it a few times, clinked the spoon against the edge of the cup, and placed it in his saucer.

"You don't mean he's—but Mr. Laemmle said he was such a spiritual fellow."

A Japanese waiter appeared and asked what Emily would have for breakfast.

"Try some citrus fruit," Bruns said. "Here we are in California, after all."

"No citrus fruit," the waiter said. "I can bring you orange juice out of a can."

"That will be fine," Emily said. "And some coffee, and toast, and an egg."

"No egg," the waiter said. "Corned beef hash."

"Excellent. Bring me canned orange juice and corned beef hash." Emily could be flexible. The waiter went away again. "So what you're telling me is that McHenry likes men."

"According to his associates at the bathhouse, yes."

"What does this mean to our investigation?"

"I think it does away with the angle of *cherchez la femme*."

"Maybe," Emily said.

"Maybe?"

"If he isn't attracted to women, it doesn't necessarily mean they aren't attracted to him."

"I s'pose you have a point. All right, Miss Daggett, you get on up to McHenry's house in the Krotona community and *cherchez* whatever you can find. If anybody bothers you, tell them you're looking for spiritual fulfillment. Hang around the community and talk to as many people as you can without letting them know what you're really interested in."

"Okay." She almost said, "Right, chief," but that was what she always used to say to Adam. May he rot. "Tell me something, Mr. Bruns. Do you know anybody in Ciudad Juárez?"

"Why?"

"I was wondering whether you could make a telephone call, maybe, and check on my husband. See whether he's still alive. That sort of thing."

"Miss Daggett. Surely you aren't hoping you're a widow."

"Certainly not."

"Adam Weiss is still alive and kicking."

"How do you know?"

"As it happens I do have a friend down there, and my friend has instructions to notify me if there is any change in the status of your husband. So far there is no change."

"Oh." She didn't have the courage to ask him what his friend had reported the unchanging status of Adam to be. Entwined with Agnes? Emily didn't want to hear about it.

"Come along, now, Miss Daggett, it's time for you to go up to Krotona and have a good look at Ross McHenry's house."

"First I must make a few adjustments to my wardrobe. Should I try to get inside?"

"Not to the point of breaking and entering, but if somebody invites you in, go ahead, always bearing in mind that if the worst has come to pass the person who invites you might be Ross McHenry's killer." Killer. She almost missed the rest of what he had to say. "Do you have carfare and lunch money?"

"Yes, thank you."

"Then I'll see you in Carl Laemmle's office at eleven o'clock."

SIX

An unassuming shirtwaist, a plain dark gray skirt, and a sober
attitude seemed to Emily to be all the disguise she would
need to pass herself off as a spiritual seeker, that and her
least extravagant hat, a little straw thing. On her way out
the door she remembered Billie Burke's window-glass
gold-rimmed pince-nez. It had fallen from the unconscious actress's lovely nose as she was being stuffed into
Agnes Gelert's steamer trunk. No one noticed it until the
boy had left with the trunk. Since the lenses weren't pre-
scription glass, and Miss Burke was by that time steaming
off to Europe, Emily had not felt obliged to return it.

She took it out of her handbag now, pinched it on her
nose, and checked her reflection in the hat-stand mirror

by the front door of the hotel. The effect was perfect. She looked as plain as a mud fence.

For all its vaunted ascetic spirituality, the Krotona community loomed over Temple Hill Drive like a collection of Moorish pleasure domes. None of the Theosophists were in sight as Emily walked uphill toward the compound. She found Ross McHenry's bungalow easily, halfway up the hill, modest and attractive in the Craftsman style, with a well-kept yard. A shirtless yard boy with muscles like slim bands of iron clipped the gumdrop-shaped shrubbery, snick, snick. When he turned so that Emily could see his face in profile she recognized him as someone she had known in New York: Vera Zinovia's cousin, Boris Ivanovich Levin.

Vera had been one of Melpomene's first stars, before she went back to Russia with her lover, Big Ed Strawfield of the Industrial Workers of the World, to attend the birth of the revolution. Emily had not heard anything from either of them since. She still remembered the pungent smell of the Greenwich Village coffeehouse where Vera had introduced her to this cousin: Turkish cigarettes, strong coffee, the sweat of ardent young Socialist students.

Boris Levin of the Moscow Art Theater was the finest actor in the western hemisphere, or so his cousin Vera claimed. At the time when Emily first met him, Boris Levin's type was wrong for the picture Melpomene was trying to cast. Still, Emily was enormously impressed by his vivid presence, his dark hair and luminous eyes. She was dying to put him in a film. It was hardly a problem that he spoke no English, for she proposed to direct him by means of gestures. Alas! By the time Melpomene Studios had a part for him, Emily no longer knew how to reach him. He had disappeared from his Greenwich Village haunts.

That Boris was in Hollywood seemed perfectly fitting. That he was trimming Ross McHenry's hedge seemed strange.

"Boris!" Emily called. "Boris Levin!"

"I beg your pardon?" He seemed to be learning the language, at least, but his accent was even thicker than Vera's, "I peck your parthen." Emily spoke to him as clearly as she could.

"I'm sure you don't remember me, but we met years ago in New York City. My husband and I were casting a moving picture. Your cousin Vera Zinovia was in it. She introduced us." Emily took off the glasses, in case that would allow him to recognize her face more easily.

"Mrs. Weiss! Of course I remember you."

"It's Miss Daggett now." She put the glasses back on.

"Oh. I'm sorry. Miss Daggett. Is something—?"

"It's quite all right. Are you still acting?"

"As well to ask if I'm still breathing. Unhappily I have no work of that sort."

"You're working here. For Mr. . . . ?"

"McHenry. Yes." He brushed a lock of dark hair out of his eyes with the back of his arm.

"What do you think of him?"

"I think he is rotten bastard. Forgive me."

"Good heavens! Why?"

Boris proceeded to tell her his tale of woe: how he and

McHenry had met at the IMP studios in New York; how McHenry had persuaded him to come to California, promising to get him a role in a picture; how instead of that, McHenry had installed him in a room over the garage and used him for a yard boy.

"Six months I work here," Boris said. "Six months. Still have I not seen the inside of a moving picture studio."

"You must feel terribly frustrated."

"Frustrated. Yes. Is good word."

"But, tell me. Have you seen Mr. McHenry lately?"

"Mr. Ross McHenry has not been home in three weeks. Let him stay away. Pfui."

"What will you do if he never comes back at all?"

"Why would he not come back? He always comes back before."

"Does he go away often?"

Boris Levin frowned, as though the idea was something he had never considered. A bead of sweat formed on his forehead and rolled into his eye. The sun was very warm; Emily was feeling it herself. At last he said, "Would you like to come inside, dear lady? I can offer you a glass of tea."

"Thank you," she said, thinking he was proposing to entertain her in his quarters over the garage. Instead of that he opened the front door to McHenry's house, using a key, and beckoned her inside.

"We drink McHenry's Lapsang souchong," Boris said. "Rotten bastard. He is owing me four weeks' pay."

Inside McHenry's house it was much cooler and there was a vaguely metallic smell. No newspapers or mail littered the tables and chairs in the living room, which was furnished with simple oak pieces in the Craftsman style. The only books in evidence were tomes on Theosophy, penned by Madam Helen Blavatsky and other adepts of the movement. A silver-framed picture of Babette de Long stared petulantly from the stone mantel, inscribed in a childish scrawl: "All my love, Babs."

"I put on kettle for tea," Boris said. Emily took advantage of his absence to look in the drawer of McHenry's writing table. Under a pack of cards and some photographs she found a manly nickel-plated gun, nothing like the pearl-handled cutie she had lifted from Billie Burke, and a small leather case, which, when opened, proved to contain a brass syringe with several detachable needles and a tube of pills. Evidently McHenry was ill.

Suddenly Emily realized what had happened to him. Deprived of his medication, he had collapsed in a coma someplace where he wasn't known—were there such places, for famous movie stars?—and lay unidentified in a hospital. Or morgue. She could hardly wait to tell Mr. Bruns. But surely Mr. Bruns had checked the hospitals and morgues on the very first day McHenry went missing.

Boris Levin's footsteps approached from the rear of the house. Quickly Emily put everything back in the drawer the way she found it. When Levin arrived carrying the tea on a tray she was standing nonchalantly in front of the stone fireplace, admiring the picture of Little Babs.

"What a pretty child," she said.

"Is one of movie people."

"She looks young enough to be his daughter."

"People come and go in this house," Boris said.

"Daughters, mistresses, charwomen, they could be anything to Mr. Ross McHenry. Or nothing. I'm sure they're nothing to me. Normally I don't come in here." He put the tray down on the writing desk. "Please to sit down. We'll talk about Mr. Ross McHenry's comings and goings, if you're really interested in hearing."

"Certainly," Emily said. "Can I see the upstairs?"

"No one is to be going upstairs," Boris said. "Not even I am to be going upstairs. Mr. Ross McHenry, famous movie star, rotten bastard, is threatening to kill me if ever I go upstairs in his house."

"Good heavens. Why?"

"Who knows? Maybe he is keeping bars of gold up there. Maybe he has slave chained to his bed."

"Surely in that case he would have you go up and feed the poor creature occasionally. Especially since he's been away for such a long time." Emily glanced at the staircase; the flight of stairs had a landing in the middle and bent back on itself, so that the top of the stairs could not be seen. "Does he have any house servants?"

"You think is big joke. Last time I tried to go upstairs Ross McHenry pulled out huge gun and offered to shoot me."

"Good heavens."

"I am not caring why. I am staying outside except when I come in and steal his tea. Yes, he had a Japanese charwoman, but she quit some time ago."

"Well, now I have to see the upstairs. It's perfectly safe; Mr. McHenry isn't here."

"You say he isn't here. At any moment he could be here."

"Then how can we dare to drink his tea?"

"I told you. Revenge."

"Well, I'm going up." She got as far as the landing before a key rattled in the lock.

McHenry. Emily ran downstairs again, picked up her guilty tea, and assumed a pose of insouciance. So he was back! Good. Now she could get busy on *Captain Jinks*. With luck she could find a part for Boris Levin in it, with that face, those eyes. It was a crime to keep him out of moving pictures. What McHenry might have had in mind, dragging this beautiful boy all the way across the continent and then making a servant out of him, Emily forbore to speculate.

But it was not McHenry at the door. When the door opened it was to reveal a thin, exotic woman, dressed in barbaric silks, wearing armloads of silver bracelets and a striped turban with a feather in it. Who could this be, letting herself in with a key, scowling at them so fiercely? Too fashionable for a charwoman, too old to be McHenry's daughter, she could have been his mistress only if he liked skinny, ill-tempered women. A smell of sandalwood clung about her. Under the turban she was sandy-haired, pale-complexioned, with eyes of a penetrating shade of green. Her eyebrow was a single line across her face.

She fastened the eyes upon Emily, and penetrated. "Who are you and what are you doing here?" Her attention was like a physical assault. Emily took a step backward.

Boris stepped between them. "Mrs. Kazanow!" he said. The hair stood up on the nape of Emily's neck. Kazanow, was it? Coincidence, perhaps. "Mrs. Alma Kazanow, may I present Miss—?" His eyes met Emily's. She nodded. Miss, yes. Call me miss. "Daggett?"

"Boris, Boris. You have your own quarters over the garage. Surely Mr. McHenry has never encouraged you to conduct your social activities in his living room." Mrs. Kazanow turned her terrible gaze to the steaming tea, perfuming the room with the fragrance of lemons and creosote.

"I'm not really here to see Mr. Levin," Emily said.

"Who, then?"

"In fact I have come to the Krotona community as a seeker." Not a complete lie, after all.

"Indeed, Miss Daggett. And for what, may I ask, do you seek?"

"Truth, Mrs. Kazanow. Spiritual truth." She unfocused her eyes behind the pince-nez and gave Mrs. Kazanow a vapid smile.

"I see. You are interested in the Krotona movement, and you know of Mr. McHenry's connection to the Esoteric Society."

"Exactly. I wish to know the esoteric secrets—the secrets of reptilians and simulism—"

"As it happens, Miss Daggett, I am the recording secretary of the local Esoteric Society. You will find me far more advanced in the secrets of Theosophy than Boris, here." She laughed, a strange false little tinkle. "You've come to the right street, but the wrong house, you see. Why don't you come with me? I can help you with any questions you may have about the Krotona community." She hooked her arm through Emily's in a sisterly fashion. And so off they went, leaving Boris alone with the tea. Whatever errand Mrs. Kazanow had let herself into the house to perform remained undone.

Mrs. Kazanow's house, across the street from Ross McHenry's, looked very similar to it, but the front entrance was not as public, being hidden from most of the street by thick, tall shrubbery planted around the Craftsman portico. To approach the front door was to step into a green cave. The clatter of doggy toenails answered the sound of Mrs. Kazanow's key in the lock, and when the door opened a huge Irish wolfhound stood before them, panting. The creature uttered a woof and moved its gaze from Mrs. Kazanow's face to Emily's, with a look of guarded interest that was almost human.

"Satan! Under the piano," Mrs. Kazanow said. The dog backed away, groveling, a courtier leaving the presence of his queen, and lay down under the grand piano. "He's only a puppy. Don't be afraid of him. He won't hurt you." Emily had not thought to be afraid of the dog, but now she wasn't sure. He continued to watch her, with mature hostility, she would have said, and not with the innocence of a puppy.

The windows were hung with blood-colored velvet trimmed with beads. The furniture was covered with strange Eastern textiles. Thick hangings blocked the view through doorways to other rooms. On a table lay an arrangement of curious playing cards. Emily had not long to wonder whether this gypsy Mrs. Kazanow was in some way related to the monster who had ruined her husband, for there on her shawl-draped piano was a picture of needle-nosed, liver-lipped Howie Kazanow himself, smiling modestly, an excellent likeness except for the absence of drool. It was inscribed: "To my dearest wife." The smoke of incense curled from a small brass pot next to the picture, suggesting that Mrs. Kazanow worshipped her own worthless husband as a minor god of some sort.

Mrs. Kazanow took off her gloves; her long bony fingers glittered with curiously fashioned rings. She offered her hand, and Emily stuck out her own hand, devoid of ornamentation. Adam's wedding ring lay in the bottom of her handbag, underneath Billie Burke's pistol.

"Welcome to Krotona," Mrs. Kazanow said. Her handclasp was damp and chilly; her rings crushed Emily's fingers to the point of pain. "So you're seeking truth."

"Spiritual truth, Mrs. Kazanow. I wish to connect with the infinite. I understand that the Theosophists have . . . the inside track." Emily batted her eyes, feeling her eyelashes brush uncomfortably against the glass of Billie Burke's pince-nez. "That is to say, the path to inner fulfillment is most clearly illuminated by the methods of Theosophy, is it not?"

Mrs. Kazanow laughed her humorless little laugh. "Indeed it is, Miss Daggett. Here we study the secret wisdom of the East. This knowledge has brought happiness to our adherents, three hundred and seventy-five of them in Krotona Hollywood alone. I'm sure you have seen for yourself the radiance in their faces, as you passed among them."

"Actually I haven't passed among very many— Radiance. Yes." In fact she hadn't seen a single soul between her streetcar stop and Ross McHenry's house. They were all in the shade somewhere, doing whatever it was that religious fanatics did first thing in the morning.

"We chant," Mrs. Kazanow said, as though reading her mind. "We practice Ayurvedic yoga. We strive for perfection in thought and action; perfect breathing and perfect circulation, perfect digestion and perfect generation, perfect voice and perfect speaking. In the morning we tend our gardens. We eat lightly of vegetable substances to purify our prana. Ah. It's gone out." She retrieved a box of jasmine incense from a drawer in her desk, placed a small cone in the brass incense burner next to Howie's picture, scratched a match on the sole of her shoe, and lit the cone. The top of the incense burner made a ting sound when Mrs. Kazanow replaced it. The smoke wafted forth. The dog sneezed and snorted.

Mrs. Kazanow resumed her description of the Theosophist program: "In the heat of the day we read the writings of Madame Blavatsky and the great scholars of Theosophy. Our time in this world is filled with clean living and spiritual work. When we pass on into the next life, our earthly remains are cremated, so as to release the astral body and spare the earth the contamination of rot. You seem tense, my dear. May I—?" She moved behind Emily, put her hands on her shoulders, and began to knead with her thumbs.

It was all that Emily could do to keep from screaming; for a mad instant she thought of knocking the woman down and running out. But after all it felt good. She let her continue, and eventually it felt quite good indeed. When Mrs. Kazanow stopped her kneading, the tension in Emily's shoulders was gone.

"Thank you," Emily said, thinking, You pervert. How dare you put your hands on my body.

"You really should consider joining our community. The practice of yoga would do you a great deal of good. The Brothers of Light know more about how to live than western materialists will ever begin to understand." And this woman was married to Howie Kazanow, that soulless money-grubber, burning incense before his picture as though he were dead? Maybe she wished he were dead. "Diet is so important. No meat, no alcohol. Only in this way can you purify your prana. And of course our adherents give everything to the cause, our cause that has brought all of us so much happiness. They have sacrificed every consideration in the outside world to work and study here, and in return they have a happiness that can scarcely be imagined by the worldly." Now it was coming, the pitch for money. This was more like a Kazanow. "Tell me about your worldly life, Miss Daggett."

How far should Emily string her along? When could she turn the conversation to the whereabouts of Ross McHenry? She put the back of her wrist to her brow like a movie heroine and said, with more truth than not, "I find myself at a crossroads, Mrs. Kazanow. I have suffered a series of dreadful betrayals. My worldly life is—" She spread her hands and shrugged.

"You need guidance."

"That might be helpful."

"Let me give you a reading."

"A reading?"

"The tarot. Sit down, won't you?" She indicated a chair at the table where the cards were spread out.

Mrs. Kazanow shuffled the cards together, gave them

to Emily to hold and cut, then dealt out three cards, face-down.

"The nine of swords," she said, turning up the first card. "Poor child, you are in despair." The picture on the card was of a woman sitting up in bed, a pretty bed covered with an attractive quilt, holding her hands over her face. Nine swords hung over the bed. "Utter desolation. Death, failure, deception—"

"Good heavens," Emily said.

Mrs. Kazanow took Emily's hand in her own. Like any good fortune-teller, she may have observed the pale line around Emily's ring finger. "Your husband is gone," she said. "Is he dead?"

"I don't really know," Emily said. "Is he?" Could it be that he was dead? Anything could happen to a man in a place like Mexico, no matter what Holbert Bruns had told her. Bruns was nothing if not a skillful liar. Would she mind if Adam were dead? Rotten bastard. She started to cry again. Where was her handkerchief? She took off Billie Burke's glasses and wiped her eyes with the back of her free hand.

"The cards have more to say." Mrs. Kazanow released her hand and turned over the second card. "The fool."

The happy young fellow in the picture carried a stick over his shoulder with a bag tied to it; his little dog frisked at his feet; he was stepping off a cliff. Though it was only a bit of pasteboard, Emily's stomach lurched. She had always been terrified of falling from heights. Was she fated to do that now? "What does it mean?"

"It's a good card," Mrs. Kazanow said. "Excellent. Your troubles will pass. You are beginning a journey."

"I hope my journey doesn't involve falling off a cliff," Emily said.

"No, no, what you see is symbolic. For example this third card"—she turned the third card over—"this is the knight of cups. Reversed."

The card, being upside-down, was easy for Emily to see. It cheered her. A knight in armor on a beautiful horse. Someone was coming to save her. Adam was coming back. What else could it mean?

Mrs. Kazanow was still staring at the card. At last she said, "You aren't what you claim to be, are you?"

"I beg your pardon?"

"What were you really doing in Ross McHenry's house?"

"I told you. Seeking the truth."

"I suspect you are a little movie fan, seeking nothing higher than to get a sight of Mr. McHenry in the flesh."

"Why, no, I—"

"I must ask you to leave the premises of the Krotona colony now. Your kind of seeker isn't welcome here." The wolfhound came out from under the piano and stood next to his mistress's chair, bristling with alertness.

"But, Mrs. Kazanow, surely . . ."

Mrs. Kazanow rang a little bell. An Asian servant appeared. "Rokurou, show Miss Daggett the door." Satan gave a long, low growl.

SEVEN

Even though Mrs. Kazanow had cast her out of the Krotona community, watching her all the way down Temple Hill Drive from her leafy doorway, Emily felt light and at one with the cosmos as she trotted toward the streetcar stop. The massage had done something good to her spine, and the handy tips were elevating. Even the tarot reading made her feel better than it was supposed to. She considered these things, boarding the streetcar. Despair is bad. Meat is bad. Drink is bad. Maybe that was why she could never get pregnant; her prana was impure. If Adam were to come back! She was still considering when the streetcar let her off at the stop nearest the IMP studios, right in front of the doorway to Feeny's Café, a low dive with a ladies' entrance.

As the trolley pulled away a crowd of drunks boiled out

the front door, punching and kicking each other. Emily stepped back, watched them roll away down Glendale Boulevard, and sighed. Imagine drinking in a bar at that hour of the day. And yet before she went to face Holbert Bruns and Carl Laemmle she could almost consider slipping into this joint through the ladies' entrance and having a quick one. If she were caught it would ruin what was left of her reputation, but what of it? As for her prana, maybe she didn't have any. Suddenly she heard the voices of women inside, singing:

"I'm *Cap*-tain Jinks of the Horse Marines, I feed my horse on corn and beans, and sport young ladies in their teens, to cut a dash in the *aaar*-my!"

"That's the stuff!" The voice could only be Etta Sweet's. The actresses from *Jinks* must be in town, inside this very bar, boisterously drunk at ten thirty in the morning. Sure enough, Emily found them sitting around a grubby table consuming a dish of pickled sausage and a pitcher of beer.

"Hello, ladies." Emily dragged a chair across the sticky floor and joined them. "What cheer?"

"No cheer is what cheer, lady," Etta said.

"We've been dumped," Wanda said.

"Stranded. We pooled the last of our money to buy this pitcher of beer," Gertrude said.

"We're all going to have to be whores now," Etta said.

"Oh, surely things can't be that bad," Emily said. "Anyway, I can pay for the beer. I have a job."

"Hurrah! She can pay for the beer!" Etta said.

"Get her a glass!" Gertrude said. "Lordy, lady, you look awful. Why are you wearing those specs?"

"No reason." Emily hastily removed the pince-nez and dropped it down the front of her dress, where it hung unseen from a black silk ribbon.

"You didn't put on any makeup this morning."

"So I didn't. An oversight."

Wanda bent toward her with a moue of sincerity and put a friendly hand on her arm. "Listen, honey, don't let that man of yours get you down. So he's gone. There'll be another one along before you know it, as long as you don't let yourself go all to hell."

"I expect you're right."

"Tell us about this job you have." Gertrude was still sober enough to focus on the important things. "Are there any more where that came from?"

"It's confidential."

Etta snorted. "You mean his wife doesn't know."

"No, really, it's a confidential assignment. So the road company of *Jinks* broke up?"

"The road company of *Jinks* was a complete flopperoo," Etta said, "thanks to the infant they hired to play Trentoni." She ate the last of the pickled sausage.

Wanda helped herself to more beer. "We came to Los Angeles and didn't even open. So now nobody has train fare home."

"Or, until you came in, the price of another pitcher, if it comes to that," Etta said.

Gertrude poured the last drop into her glass. "It has come to that. *Garçon!*"

The barman, scrawny, pop-eyed, wearing a soiled apron, shambled in from the barroom and gave them all the look, as if he thought they had already taken up Etta's second-choice profession. "Another pitcher," Gertrude said.

"Please," Emily added. The barman grunted and went away.

"The only one who got out alive from the fiasco in Flagstaff was Little Babs herself. She has a job waiting for her at one of those new movie studios."

"I heard they were making a movie out of *Captain Jinks* and hired her to play Trentoni again after her triumphant performance in Flagstaff," Wanda said.

"I feel sorry for whoever has to direct her," Gertrude said. "As an actress she stinks on ice." She smiled at the barman as he returned with a full pitcher.

"I'm afraid that would be me," Emily said, and paid the man.

"What?!" Etta said.

Wanda said, "You're directing a movie? Wait a minute. What's confidential about that?"

"Er, certain aspects. Never mind that. Would you like your old parts back? No lines to learn; it's a movie. I can speak to Mr. Laemmle about it."

They cheered; general hilarity reigned at the table; beer and pickled sausages flowed in abundance for another half hour. At five minutes of eleven Emily remembered her appointment at the studio. She gave the actresses some money for a hotel room and told them to meet her at IMP the following afternoon. "Be ready for screen tests."

"Never readier," Gertrude said. They all jumped up and ran out, leaving on the dirty table a copy of the early edition of the *Los Angeles Morning Tribune*. Emily turned it over. Across the top, the headline screamed:

ROSS MCHENRY BEATEN TO DEATH.

McHenry's body, according to the newspaper story, had been discovered by some boys playing under the Santa Monica Pier, and identified by a label in his clothing. Too bad, too bad, Emily had so been looking forward to meeting him. Too bad, the end of a handsome man and his brilliant movie career. Still, a bright side: Emily could now begin work on *Captain Jinks of the Horse Marines,* the real reason she was in Hollywood. Into each life some sun must shine.

Emily still had the *Tribune* tucked under her arm when she took a chair next to Holbert Bruns in the waiting room outside of Carl Laemmle's office. She still had pickled sausage and beer on her breath, too, but with luck neither Bruns nor Laemmle would get close enough to notice the impurity of her prana.

"I suppose you've seen this," she said, handing Bruns the paper. "I guess this is the end of the detective part of my job. They found him. It's been nice working with you, Mr. Bruns, I want you to know that."

Bruns glanced at her newspaper and shrugged. "I'll see your bulldog edition and raise you a late city." He produced another version of the same newspaper, which proclaimed, ROSS MCHENRY KILLED IN TRAGIC DIVING ACCIDENT.

"How is this possible?"

"The wonders of modern typesetting."

"Carl Laemmle's influence?"

"Uncle Carl has a lot of influence. As for your being off the case—"

"McHenry was diving?"

"He was certainly very wet."

"What actually happened to him? Was it suicide?" Thank God she was out of it now.

"Not unless he was able to beat his own head in, drive himself to the beach, and throw himself into the Pacific Ocean with a weight tied around his leg. Who said you were off the case? You're off the case when Carl Laemmle says so. Then you can direct your movie."

Emily folded her hands in her lap and stared into the middle distance. What she was viewing with her mind's eye was a rotted corpse, a few tattered scraps of clothing still clinging to the bones of it, a chain around the leg attached perhaps to an anchor. Instead of a handsome laughing man who looked good without his shirt, beloved of a million women, a sad dead body.

Murdered, furthermore. A murder case, and here she was pretending to be a detective.

It was time to abandon this enterprise. How sweet now was the prospect of washing dishes and slinging hash, a perfectly safe occupation, where even if she did happen to come in contact with murderers from time to time, there would never be any reason for them to come after her. She could just give them their hash and take their money, and after that watch them go out the door. Whereas, if she had to be a detective, they might think it appropriate to beat her head in, drive her to the beach, and throw her in the Pacific Ocean with a weight tied around her leg. "Mr. Bruns, I can't continue with this."

"With what?" He took his pipe out of his pocket.

"I'm going to have to leave your employ. I can't deal with murders."

"I don't see why not." He scratched a match on the sole of his boot and it took fire. "You were superb in Fort Lee."

"I was fighting for my husband's life."

"And see what it got you." He held the match to his pipe and puffed.

"I beg your pardon—!"

He shrugged. "Well, if you can't you can't, Miss Daggett. I respect your wishes in this matter." He shook the match; the flame went out. "But I know that whatever you may think of yourself you aren't a coward, and I know you'll come with me now to see Carl Laemmle and tell him in person why you're quitting."

"Of course." Only people like Adam sent telegrams to weasel out of things.

"A darned shame, too, with that picture all lined up for you to direct." He sniffed. "Say, have you been drinking beer, Miss Daggett?" As he spoke these words the glass door to the reception area swung open and Howie Kazanow strolled in, bug-eyed, his ears flapping.

"Mrs. Weiss! Drinking beer at this hour, are we? How very nice to see you." Kazanow peeled off one of his flawless kidskin gloves and offered her his hand.

"I don't believe we've met," Emily said.

"Howie Kazanow," he said. "I'm a friend of your husband's."

"I don't know you and I must insist that you stop annoying me."

"So who's this fellow? Your newest paramour?"

"Excuse me, Mr. Bruns," she said, and went to look for the ladies' room, somewhere down the long corridor lined with posters of movies directed by other people. Some of those posters could say directed by Emily Daggett. As a director she would have jobs to give her actress friends, who might starve or worse if she didn't keep her promises to them. As a director she would be able to rise above the taunts of Howie Kazanow and his ilk. All she would have to do is solve the murder of Ross McHenry, in a strange city where anyone you met could be a killer. A simple matter.

When Emily returned to Carl Laemmle's reception area, her brow cooled by the application of cold tap water and her passions somewhat calmed, she found Kazanow deeply engaged in conversation with Holbert Bruns. She took a seat on the other side of Bruns. Kazanow looked at her anyway.

"Get me a cup of coffee, will you, sweetheart?"

"Are you addressing me?"

"Sure, toots."

"I'm a movie director, you odious person. I don't fetch coffee."

The lovely Millie came out of the Great Man's office and told Kazanow he could go in. Away he went, to Emily's relief.

"How could you talk to that disgusting man?" she said to Bruns.

"If you're going to be a detective, Miss Daggett, you can't run away from your enemies. You can't stop speaking to them. You must get as close to them as you can and listen to everything they have to say."

"I can't imagine Howie Kazanow having anything to say that I would want to hear."

"That's your mistake," he said.

She huffed, she sniffed, she plucked at the sleeves of her shirtwaist, and at last she said, "What did he say?"

"He's going into partnership with Carl Laemmle."

"Too bad for Mr. Laemmle. He makes an evil partner."

"Up in the hills there's a huge ranch. Mr. Laemmle and his associates in the Universal Film Manufacturing Company are buying it for a movie studio, the biggest in the world. They are going to call it Universal City. Mr. Kazanow wants a piece of it, and he plans to use the assets of Melpomene Studios for capital."

"Oh! That's my money! I worked for that money for five long years, no time off, no holidays, hardly any sleep—" She would have burst into tears if she were by herself, or if she had remembered to bring her handkerchief, or if there were no chance of Kazanow coming out of Mr. Laemmle's office to gloat over her misery.

Holbert Bruns patted her shoulder. "You don't really want to back out of our deal with Mr. Laemmle, now, do you, Miss Daggett? What would you do for a living if you did that?"

"I thought I'd get a job waiting tables, Mr. Bruns."

"Good idea. Then if Kazanow told you to get him a cup of coffee, you'd have to do it."

Several seconds went by while this unpleasant thought sank in. Bruns nursed his pipe and watched her out of the corner of his eye.

"Well, then, what the hell," she said. "I might as well be a detective and get killed by a murderer as die of humiliation."

"That's the spirit," he said. "But I won't let you get killed, Miss Daggett. I'll never ask you to do anything dangerous. You leave the dangerous stuff to me. All you have to do is go a few places and ask a few questions." He was close enough to her so that she could see the tiny individual whiskers where they grew out of his face, close enough to smell not only his pipe tobacco but also the soap he had used in his bath. It made her feel dizzy. Later she realized this was the moment when she forgot what a liar Holbert Bruns was, and how she could never really trust him.

EIGHT

"**Drop the investigation? Oh, goodness,** no, children," Carl Laemmle said. "By no means are you to drop the investigation simply because Ross McHenry has been found dead."

"You want us to solve the murder, then?" Emily said.

"There was no murder. No reason to try to solve it." The Great Man frowned, shuffled some papers on his desk.

"No murder," Emily said.

"Miss Daggett, perhaps you don't know it, but our industry here depends on the good pleasure not only of a huge general public but of hundreds of government officials, in this country and even in Europe and Asia. Selling a movie is not like selling a book. You write a book, people can choose to read it or not, and then only if they can read

English. You make a movie, anyone can see it, people with impressionable minds, little children—"

"Well, yes, I know that, but—"

"You may not be aware of the Sims Act that was passed in 1912. Boxing pictures can no longer be legally transported across state lines."

"But that's—"

"All because of that colored boy, Jack Johnson."

"Beat up a white man," Bruns explained.

"But—"

"Yes," Carl Laemmle went on, "he defeated Jim Jeffries in fourteen rounds. They got it all on film. The Patents Trust stood to make a lot of money on that picture until the people started rioting. Impressionable minds, you see."

"But—"

"And that was only part of it, the fights. It got around that Johnson was overly friendly with white girls."

"But—"

"You have to be careful what gets around about the people who appear in your pictures. Because the government reserves the right to ban them. The Postmaster. The Interstate Commerce Commission. The Chicago Board of Censors. The City of Boston. Moral depravity kills pictures."

Emily was having trouble following Laemmle's logic. "Is it an act of moral depravity to be murdered?"

"It is in Boston. So, no murder. But if the police should happen to become interested, or members of the press, they might go to McHenry's house and look around. I want you to get there before them. Anything you find that might reflect badly on Ross McHenry, anything that would ruin his reputation, or get his pictures banned, I want you to get rid of it."

"Such as—?" Emily said. Bruns didn't say anything. It struck her that Bruns already knew what Mr. Laemmle was talking about.

"Excuse my frankness, Miss Daggett. Ross McHenry slept with men." Mr. Laemmle shrugged. "There may have been other things."

"Other things he slept with?" His blankie, maybe, or little pieces of fur— Holbert Bruns glanced at her and then at Mr. Laemmle, a frown line between his brows. Could Mr. Laemmle have known about Ross McHenry and the men all along, and failed to mention it to Bruns?

"Other things he did," Mr. Laemmle said. "Things that might be against the law, or things we don't want people to know about."

"We'll know what you mean when we see it, sir," Bruns said. "You can safely leave this in our hands." He seemed to feel that the interview was over, and turned to go, but Emily's main concern had not been addressed.

She spoke up about it. "And after that I can start work on *Captain Jinks*?"

"We'll see how it goes," Mr. Laemmle said. "We have to bury the man first. Of course the studio will arrange a funeral. The women of America will want to bid him farewell. And then forget it. There was no murder."

"You're going to bury him?" Emily said. "What about his relatives?"

"He had none that we know of." A soft knock at the door. "Yes?"

One of the Laemmle nephews put his head in. "McHenry's funeral is at sundown today, Uncle Carl."

"How could that be? I haven't finished planning it yet."

"The Los Angeles City Morgue released the body to the Krotona community last night. They're staging the funeral at the auditorium of the Masonic Temple."

"Why them?"

"Dunno. The morgue guy wouldn't tell me without I let him have a screen test. Also I can't cancel the flowers."

"Why not?"

"The florist already delivered them to the chapel in Hollywood Cemetery. You want me to get some of the fellows to move them to the Masonic Temple?"

"No. Let the chapel have them. The hell with the Masonic Temple. Mr. Bruns, get over to the city morgue as soon as you finish cleaning out McHenry's house and find out how we lost control of his body."

"Miss Daggett can handle the morgue, sir. I have a lunch date with Miss Hester Mink."

"Her. Poison her while you're at it," Laemmle said.

"I'm planning to give her an angle on McHenry's death for today's column."

"She believes what you tell her?" Emily was astonished.

"I get her to drag it out of me. It's an art."

"He's worth every penny I pay him," Laemmle said. "My actors should be so good. You should be so good," he said to the nephew, still hanging in the doorway. "Go tell everybody to be at the funeral. Everybody. You, too. Black suits." The nephew closed the door. "So much for that, then. But after McHenry is planted we still have to finish *Dark Star of India,* and, as you know, we no longer have a leading man."

"Perhaps I can help you there," Emily said.

"How?"

"This morning I ran into an actor I used to know on the East Coast. He's between engagements, a fine actor, handsome and photogenic." At least, Emily supposed Boris was a fine actor. Vera said he was a fine actor. Vera's opinions were trustworthy most of the time. Certainly he would look good on camera.

"What's his name?" Mr. Laemmle said.

"Boris Ivanovich Levin."

Holbert Bruns stared at her.

"Tell him I'll give him a screen test," Mr. Laemmle said. "We'll see. Of course the monicker will have to go."

Bruns was not happy. "But—"

"Get up to McHenry's house now. Get Eddie to take you." Mr. Laemmle flapped his hand at them and turned his attention to something on his desk.

As soon as they were out of Mr. Laemmle's sight, Bruns grabbed Emily by the arm and began to heap recriminations on her head. "Boris Levin? You want to make a movie star out of Boris Levin? McHenry's yard boy! Don't you understand that he's probably the man who killed McHenry?"

"No, I don't. I don't understand any such thing."

Bruns opened his mouth to argue, but Mr. Laemmle's nephew appeared and asked if they needed anything.

"We're fine," Bruns said.

"Fine," Emily said. To have a fight in the hallway outside Mr. Laemmle's office would be impolitic. Maybe they could fight later.

Eddie the chauffeur refused to take them up to Krotona, protesting that the Cadillac was out of commission. "Take that one, the keys are in it," he said, waving his polishing rag in the direction of an open two-seater, a nice little Hispano-Suiza. He turned away from them and bent over to rub the bright work of the Cadillac, presenting them with a view of his well-muscled and smartly uniformed rump. The rag he was using appeared to be a tattered bit of old uniform pants, khaki with black braid. Thrifty fellow.

Emily settled herself in the passenger seat while Bruns went around to the front of the car. Unlike the Cadillac limousine, the Hispano-Suiza had to be cranked to get it started. As soon as the engine began thrumming and shaking, Bruns jumped in and pulled the car out onto Glendale Boulevard.

They hadn't gone but a few blocks before Bruns took up the cudgels again. So there was to be a fight. "If you think Boris Levin is harmless simply because he's a handsome smooth talker, you're being naïve, Miss Daggett."

"I don't want to tell you what you're being, Mr. Bruns." A horse and wagon pulled out in front of the car. Bruns jammed on the brakes. Emily thought, grabbing her hat, I could drive better than this if I knew how to drive. She should have learned to drive years ago. She wouldn't have to drive to be a movie director, of course, but if she were going to continue in the detective business she would need her own transportation. Adam was a terrible driver, aggressive, selfish, with no understanding of the machine he was driving, pretty much the same way he lived his life generally. He, too, would start fights with Emily as soon as he got into traffic, and the madder he got the worse he drove. The car would swerve toward telephone poles and bridge abutments until Emily feared for her life.

Holbert Bruns wasn't Adam. He might fight with her in cars but he did not fly off the handle. "Who do you like for the killer, then, if not Mr. Levin?" he said, perfectly cool.

"Howie Kazanow's wife."

"What makes you think Howie Kazanow's wife—?"

"She lives across the street."

"They're neighbors. An excellent motive."

"She let herself in with a key while I was there talking to Boris. Doesn't that mean—"

"Oh, now you're calling him Boris. Very intimate. Are you saying you were inside McHenry's house with Boris Levin? Alone?"

"I was, and I was getting a good look at the inside of the house until this horrible woman let herself in with a key and began to threaten me."

"She threatened you?"

"Or she menaced me. Anyway she was nasty. She took me home with her and gave me a back rub."

"You're not making sense, Miss Daggett." He did something with the gearshift and the clutch as they headed up the hill; the car was growling. Emily could learn to do that, maybe, if she watched him carefully. Step on the clutch, wiggle the gearshift. . . . "You're obsessed with the Kazanows because Howard Kazanow tricked your husband out of his movie company."

"Our movie company."

"Your movie company. But your judgment is warped, don't you think?"

"No."

"Just the same, be careful of Boris Levin. Even though you think you can trust him."

"I trust everybody," she said. "I trust them to do what I've seen them do before."

His smile was grim. "A pragmatist, Miss Daggett?"

"It's the New England way. As a pragmatist, I wonder whether it matters who killed Ross McHenry. If Mr. Laemmle is paying us to forget about it."

"Mr. Laemmle is paying us so that he can forget about it. Our job is to keep it quiet. We need to know who killed Ross McHenry, because we can't keep something quiet if we don't know exactly what it is we're supposed to be hushing up."

"I see. I think."

Mrs. Kazanow's driveway, across the street from Ross McHenry's bungalow, was empty of cars. Emily hoped that this was a sign that the tiresome woman wasn't home. In case she was, or in case some other of McHenry's neighbors might be peering through their venetian blinds, they parked the studio's car around the corner. Bruns said that they must approach Ross McHenry's house cautiously.

"How? I mean, how does a real detective sneak up on a

house in a busy neighborhood in the full glare of the California sun?"

"With his chin up," Bruns said, "walking briskly. You're McHenry's sister. I'm, say, your husband. We have every right to be here. Allow me to take your arm, my dear. That's the way." As usual, the touch of his hand on her arm was vaguely disturbing, even through a layer of cloth.

They knocked at the front door. No one answered. Boris Levin was nowhere in evidence, nor did he answer their knock on the door to his apartment over the garage. While Bruns stood glaring at her, Emily scribbled a note and slipped it into the letter slot, telling Boris to come to the studio for a screen test tomorrow morning. If Bruns disapproved of Boris it was just too bad. The man was an actor, an artist. Emily required his art.

They went around through the wash yard in the back and banged on McHenry's kitchen door. Still no answer.

"Never mind; we'll simply break and enter," Bruns said. He applied a picklock to the kitchen door; they broke and entered. "Keep your gloves on. No fingerprints, you see."

A quick glance around the kitchen revealed nothing that looked bad for McHenry, unless sour milk counted. The iceman had brought fresh ice recently, and someone, probably Boris, had been regularly emptying the drip pan underneath, but inside the icebox the milk had gone bad. Bruns found the door to the back stairs next to a row of cupboards.

"Come on," he said. "We'll check the upstairs first."

On the forbidden second floor, abuzz with houseflies, they found two bedrooms and a bathroom. There was a strong metallic smell that made Emily even more uneasy than the smell of sour milk. Bruns searched the bathroom while Emily looked around in what must have been the guest room, frilly and girly, with an empty chest of drawers ready for the clothes of guests. No abandoned underwear or suggestive objects.

Across the hall was McHenry's own bedroom, thoughtfully decorated in green and brown in the Craftsman tradition. The walls were papered with a small print of stems and leaves surmounted by a frieze of stylized hunting scenes. The windows were hung with coarse linen curtains and looked out on the hillside rising behind the house, the backyards of the neighbors. Whoever cleaned had failed to remove some black scuff marks, heel marks, Emily would have said, on the windowsill. The furniture was the heavy quartersawn oak that McHenry favored. No indication of slaves having been tied to the bed.

The smell was getting worse. Emily still couldn't tell what it was, not consciously, but some deep part of her felt revulsion and terror. She wanted to leave.

"Boris told me he wasn't allowed to come up here," Emily said. "He told me Ross McHenry pulled a gun on him once and threatened to kill him if he tried to go upstairs."

"Must have been someone up here he didn't want him to see," Bruns said.

"Maybe that was it." McHenry's clothes had been put away in an orderly fashion. His suits hung in the closet. His linens lay carefully folded in the chest of drawers. In a dish on top of the chest lay his cuff links and watch, still waiting for the wrists that would never return.

On the wall over the bed hung a tasteful charcoal drawing of a male nude. "Take that down," Bruns said.

"Why? Is it someone we know?"

"No, but it looks queer. What if the newspapers brought a photographer in here? It might make the wrong impression on the public mind."

Emily unhooked the picture wire from the hook on the wall and put the picture on the floor while Bruns searched through McHenry's rolled-up socks. The picture's absence left a pale square on the leafy wallpaper. "What shall I do about that? It calls attention to itself."

"You're right," Bruns said. "Here's what you can do. Draw a pair of plus fours on the fellow and hang it up again."

"That would be obscene."

"I suppose it would. Well, put it back, then. We'll just call it art."

"No, we'll move it to a less suggestive place. I'll hang another one over the bed. This one, for instance. A harmless bouquet of flowers."

"Strange thing for a man to hang in his bedroom," Bruns said, and turned to rummage in the drawer to the nightstand.

"Probably some woman hung it there. It doesn't even belong in this spot, if you want my opinion. It unbalances the whole room, and the colors don't match. Anyway, I'll just put it over the—" She pulled the still life of flowers away from the wall. The picture was hiding a huge stain, an explosion of dried blood.

NINE

"Oh, my heavens." Emily put the picture back.

Holbert Bruns paused in his searching activities. "What?"

"A huge bloodstain. This must be where—"

"You aren't going to faint or anything, are you?"

"Don't be silly." She picked up the orange throw rug, which didn't match the décor either; more blood underneath, black, soaked deep into the wood. This was where the smell was coming from. "I don't think so, anyway." She turned her face toward the door and took a deep breath. "At least I won't scream."

Bruns hung the nude back up again. "So this is where McHenry got it." He glanced around the bedroom, at the bed, at the wall, with a new attitude, as though the room where a man had been murdered was more deserving of respectful attention than an ordinary bedroom. He lifted the flower picture off the wall and put it on the floor, then went to the doorway and stared for a long time at the splatter.

"What?"

"Bullet holes there. I'm working out the trajectory. McHenry gets up out of the other side of the bed, killer shoots across the bed at him, blood on the wall, he falls, blood on the floor. I think you're right about the picture; that and the rug, too, came from someplace else." He went around the bed and replaced the picture. "We'd better leave the room the way we found it. Nothing in the nightstand but nose drops, headache remedies, nail clippers, and tweezers. Funny he didn't keep a gun."

"He kept it downstairs."

"Oh, really? Where?"

"In the living room, in the drawer of his writing desk, along with some little pills and a syringe."

"Let's have a look, then." Back in the hallway Bruns stooped down, picked something up from the floor, stood looking at whatever it was in the palm of his hand. "Okay," he said, and slipped whatever it was into his watch pocket.

"Okay what?"

"Shell casings. Four of 'em. Looks like thirty-two caliber. Let's go see this gun of yours."

"My gun?"

"No, McHenry's gun that you found downstairs. Do you carry a gun, Miss Daggett?"

"Sometimes I find it useful."

"You once shot my associate in the foot, as I recall. Are you carrying it now?"

"Of course."

"Loaded?"

"I think so. Actually I'm not sure how this one works; it's not the same one I used to shoot Mr. Grogan." She took it out of her handbag and waved it at him.

"Will you look at that. A Remington-Smoot gambler's five-shot." He took it from her. "You hardly see those anymore."

"It doesn't seem to have any trigger."

"It has a spur trigger, Miss Daggett. It drops down when you cock the hammer." He gave it back; she started to pull the hammer back to see what would happen. "No, no! Put it away. I'll show you later. You need some practice with that for your own safety, and also some instructions on how to pick a lock, since we're going to be working together. I'm surprised at you, being so ill-prepared. While you're looking for the trigger of that thing someone could take it away from you and hurt you."

"Oh." There was nothing else to say. Emily hadn't given a whole lot of thought to Billie Burke's gun. It was true that she had no idea how it worked.

They went down the front stairs to the living room. McHenry's gun, if it had been his, was no longer in the drawer.

"What did it look like?" Bruns said.

"Big, sort of square, gray metal, black hand grips—"

"Was it a revolver like yours?"

"Not a revolver. And the one in the drawer had a big trigger and a what-do-you-call-it, a trigger guard."

"Probably a Browning semiautomatic, like mine." He unholstered his firearm and showed it to her.

"Pretty much like it," she said.

The gun went back in the shoulder holster. "Let's see what else we—aha!" The case with the syringe and pills was still in the drawer. Bruns put it in his pocket.

The sudden rattle of a key in the lock sent them diving behind the oak settle, which was piled with enough embroidered cushions to keep them from being seen hiding behind the back slats. Emily discovered a crack between two cushions that gave her a good view of the front door. As she watched, the door swung open, and there in the doorway, leaning on her cane, stood the woman who had been so kind to her in the ladies' lounge of the Weatherford Hotel in Flagstaff. She was dressed severely in black with a black veil thrown back over the brim of her hat.

The woman shut the door and peered around the room. Emily held her breath. Holbert Bruns took her hand and squeezed it. Having evidently seen what she was looking for, the woman went straight to the mantelpiece, using the cane, thump-click, thump-click, took the silver-framed picture of Little Babs, and went out again, closing the door softly.

"Who was that? Could you see?" Bruns whispered.

"A woman I last saw in Flagstaff. I don't know who she is."

"Flagstaff?"

"She took Little Babs's picture from the mantelpiece."

"Was it Babs's mother?"

"How could it be Babs's mother? That woman was very kind to me in Flagstaff. I've always heard that Babs's mother was a monster." She went back to the desk drawer. "I wonder what happened to that gun." There were packs of cards, a stack of snapshots taken on a beach, loose poker chips, aged rubber bands, worn pencil stubs, slips of scrap paper with letters and numbers on it. No gun.

"Never mind the gun," Bruns said. "Deal with it later. I have to meet Hester Mink for lunch, and you have to get over to the morgue."

"What about the rest of the stuff in this drawer? It might be full of clues."

"Take anything you think we can use and let's go." Emily grabbed double handfuls of snapshots, the slips of paper, and pencil stubs and stuffed them in her bag. As she stepped through the swinging door to the kitchen the front doorknob turned; once again a key rattled.

They bolted. The kitchen door swung shut behind them as the front door of the house banged open. From the living room came the low growl of Satan the hellhound.

The booming voice of Alma Kazanow called out: "Whoever you are, I know you're in here. The police are on their way." With a snarl the dog rushed the swinging door.

Bruns and Emily were outside by then, sprinting for the car.

———

They said very little during the drive to the Los Angeles City Morgue, each lost in thought. Holbert Bruns frowned and drummed on the steering wheel with his fingers. Emily sat with her gloved hands in her lap, wondering whether it was really okay not to call the police. All that blood, all that evidence, surely the police would be very interested. The press would be interested, too, of course. Mr. Laemmle would be horrified, but only if the news got out. Evidently Holbert Bruns really believed what he said, that there was no useful law west of the Pecos. Now he was making himself an accessory to a murder. Perhaps not for the first time. And what of Emily? Should she worry about going to jail?

When Emily got out of the car Bruns told her what streetcar to take to get back to the studio, where she was to meet him afterward. "You can get a bite to eat at the commissary," he said.

Eating was the last thing on her mind, with the smell of Ross McHenry's blood still in her nose. She was thankful not to be forced to go all the way down into the depths of the morgue where the bodies were kept to find the information she sought, although even at the reception desk there were terrible smells: disinfectant, death, decay. The young man behind the desk must have been so used to the atmosphere that he no longer noticed it. The smile he gave her was like a breath of fresh air in itself. Another good-looking young person in another menial job. She told him she had come to inquire about the body of Ross McHenry.

"Did you know him?" he said, and, "Are you in the movie business?"

"No and yes," she said. She gave him a dazzling smile. "IMP Pictures. I'm a director."

His face glowed with handsomeness. Discover me, he seemed to say. "Mr. McHenry's body is no longer here."

"I know. Can you tell me to whom it was released?"

He made a show of looking it up in a ledger, although Emily suspected he knew perfectly well off the top of his head. It was Ross McHenry they were talking about, after all, not Joe Bindlestiff. He found the page. "McHenry, Ross. Released to the next of kin."

"And who was that?"

"His daughter."

Ross McHenry had a daughter? "Did she show you any identification?"

"Oh, yes. She had a British passport, and her name was . . . let me see . . . Barbara McHenry."

"What did she look like?"

"Don't know. She wore a long black veil."

"Well, then, what did she sound like?"

"She never spoke. She had a strange-looking woman with her who did all the talking. Weird clothes. Thin. Wore a turban. I thought maybe she was a gypsy or something."

"Did she have an accent?"

"No. Her voice was deep for a woman."

Alma Kazanow. "Speaking of clothing, could you tell me what Mr. McHenry was wearing when he . . . er . . ."

"By the way, my name is Henry Gordon. You can reach me here." He handed her a visiting card with a telephone number scrawled on it in pencil. "Do you think you can get me a screen test?"

Nice shoulders, well-shaped hands, beautiful eyes, a certain sparkle of merriment that would photograph well. "I might possibly be able to."

"Ah. Possibly, then, he was wearing a blue silk thing. Whaddaya call it, brocade. Might have been a smoking jacket, might have been a robe, before it rotted all to pieces in the ocean. Had his name in it, anyway. Lucky it did, too, because the skull was so badly—"

"Thank you. You've been very helpful." Emily rummaged in her handbag. "Tell me, are morgue clerks allowed to accept tips?"

"I'd rather have a screen test."

She put his card away. "I can't promise you anything, but I'll see what I can do, Mr. Gordon."

Getting a bite to eat at the commissary, listlessly picking at a plateful of macaroni and cheese, Emily sat by the entrance to wait for Holbert Bruns. There she had a chance to observe a flock of little actresses lined up at the door to the wardrobe department out in the hallway, requisitioning black mourning garments. They seemed excited at the prospect of attending McHenry's funeral. None of them looked very sad. Two of the IMP directors, in black suits smelling slightly of mothballs, brushed past Emily on their way to the food counter; they didn't look very sad either. There was a kind of energy in the air. The whole studio seemed to be pulling itself together to make an effort, or create a particular impression.

Holbert Bruns came in waving a copy of the evening

Examiner. He, too, was dressed in black and in a high state of liveliness. Emily planned to attend the funeral in the dark gray skirt she had put on that morning. The black hat with the raven's wing would do well enough. She was not excited to be going, but rather a little depressed.

"Here it is, Miss Daggett." He placed the paper in front of her, folded to exhibit Hester Mink's column.

ROSS MCHENRY SUICIDE
MOVIE IDOL DIES FOR LOVE

"Good heavens," Emily said. Bruns planted himself in the chair next to her, too close for comfort as usual; their breath mingled. Did he do that on purpose, or was he totally unaware? He read her the column while she choked down her meal.

"Listen to this. 'Your correspondent has discovered that the recently deceased star of IMP Studios did not die by accident. Sources say he did away with himself for love of his beautiful costar, who spurned his off-screen advances. Brokenhearted, he dived off a cliff into the Pacific Ocean, where he hit his head and was killed.'"

"You got Hester Mink to write that by buying her lunch? That was quick work."

"I led her to believe that it was a story Mr. Laemmle wanted to hush up. She wrote it up as I sat there protesting, then rushed to the telephone and called it in just in time for the deadline. Laemmle will love it. Marilyn Slater's pictures ought to attract a huge audience now."

"A huge audience of ghouls."

"Well, you know what they say. Nobody ever went broke underestimating the public taste. What did they tell you at the morgue?"

"Ross McHenry's body was released to his daughter, Barbara McHenry. She identified herself with a British passport. Alma Kazanow was with her when she went to claim her father's remains, by the way. All that was left of his clothing when he was found was a rag of blue silk damask, maybe a robe, maybe a smoking jacket."

"McHenry had a daughter?"

"She claimed to be his daughter."

"Barbara McHenry from England. Interesting. I suppose McHenry must have been English. Funny nobody ever mentioned it."

"Did he speak with an English accent?"

"I don't know. I never heard him speak. Let's ask Marilyn." Miss Slater was at that moment emerging in triumph from the wardrobe room, having secured the best-looking black dress in the place, with a neckline just north of indecency and barely a touch of sequins. Emily knew her at once, having seen five or six of her movies. She was shorter than she seemed on-screen, with blonder and less natural-looking hair. "Marilyn!" Bruns called. "Come here a minute, please."

"Whaddaya want, gumshoe?"

"Tell us something about Ross McHenry. Was he English?"

"English?"

"Did he speak with a limey accent?"

"Ross? Naw. He talked like me. Or maybe more like King Baggot. Hey! King!"

The famous actor-director emerged from the wardrobe room and joined them, brushing dust from the brim of a black top hat. "What can I do for you, Marilyn?"

"Did Ross McHenry talk with an English accent?"

"Not that I ever noticed." He put the hat on; it was a good fit. Bruns returned his attention to the newspaper.

So there was no telling where the British daughter had come from. But Alma Kazanow had gone with her to pick up the body. Why? "Do either of you know Alma Kazanow?" Emily said.

"Howie's wife," Marilyn said. "I've heard of her, is about all."

Baggot said, "I went to a few dinner parties at their beach house before she parted from Howie. She was still a sensible woman then, except for the occasional séance."

"Séance?" Emily said.

"Yes, she turned out the lights after dinner and knocked on the table. It wasn't anything. Everybody did it in those days."

"I see." Everybody in California, maybe. Emily had never encountered the practice in New York.

"Since that time I understand that she has gone completely nuts, dabbling in Los Angeles real estate and trying to turn herself into a gypsy fortune-teller. She used to come to the studio and pester Ross McHenry while they were filming his pictures. Do you remember that, Marilyn?"

"Was that woman Alma Kazanow?" Marilyn said. "God. She made the most embarrassing scenes."

"She arranged Mr. McHenry's funeral, or her Theosophist friends did," Emily said. "I'm not sure why."

"Maybe she plans to reanimate his body so she can pester him some more," Baggot said.

"Seems unlikely," Bruns said. "Not enough left to work with by the time they found him."

"Cremate him, then," Emily said.

"Why do you think that?"

"She told me the Theosophists cremate their dead."

Bruns folded the newspaper, enormously interested. "You don't say."

TEN

In later years Ross McHenry's seeing-off would be remembered as the first of the great Hollywood funerals. Thirty thousand people showed up, most of them fans, most of them women, way too many to get inside the Masonic Temple. The noise was deafening, a sound like a huge flock of chattering birds, mixed with sobbing, occasional screams, and the cries of peanut and lemonade vendors.

Somewhere inside the temple Holbert Bruns was detecting things while Emily waited on the sidewalk, along with the fans, for the hearse to arrive. His last instructions to her before he disappeared were to look sad, mix with the crowd, and keep her eyes peeled for anyone who might be McHenry's daughter. No need, he said, to try to keep the Theosophists from cremating the body; his belief was that the police already knew it was murder, and had been paid not to care.

Emily suspected that was Pinkerton talking. Her own plan was not to count on the indifference of the law, but to keep her head down and perform her assigned duties as quietly as possible. "Okay. Tell me again. What is it you want me to do?"

"Just take notice of what goes on." So she did. Emily hadn't been to many funerals in her life, being so far away from Eastport when her relatives began to die off, but even with no basis for comparison she suspected that this particular funeral was deeply strange.

On the steps outside, two cameramen had set up to record the proceedings, if not for posterity, at least for next week's moving picture audiences. Carl Laemmle appeared with three of his nephews and passed through the Moorish gates. A throng of movie actors and actresses swirled along behind him, all dressed in black, the men with their black armbands, the women with runny mascara streaking their fresh young cheeks.

One would have thought from the way he carried himself, beaming at all the peasants, that Mr. Laemmle was in charge of the whole affair. He had certainly planned to be. Bruns said he had tried to reserve a plot at Hollywood Memorial Cemetery, engage the cathedral dean to read the rites in St. Paul's, and hire a sculptor to do a marble memorial. The only successful part of his plan was the funny business he arranged with the Los Angeles district attorney to release the body without an autopsy or an inquest. But, alas! They didn't release it to him.

Somehow the hearse managed to get through the packed streets, closed for blocks around by the Los Angeles police. As it pulled up to the curb, the horses rolling their eyes nervously, a drum began to beat. The crowd fell silent, even the peanut vendors and purveyors of lemonade. The pallbearers, most of them Theosophists judging by their deep, soulful eyes, pasty complexions, scraggly beards, and unfashionable clothes, wrestled the coffin, a pine box decorated with heathen symbols, out of the back of the hearse. They seemed to have trouble lifting it onto their shoulders.

A woman standing next to Emily elbowed her in the ribs and murmured, "Look at those pantywaists. No alcohol, no meat, what can you expect?"

"Excuse me?" Emily turned to see a short person in a hat that was a shade too merry for a funeral, even a funeral conducted by weird idolaters. She held a stenographer's pad and pencil, and she was writing things down.

Emily followed the pallbearers; the writing woman fell in behind her. The crowd of mourners parted to let them go up the long walk between the avenue of palms, under the fantastical Moorish archway, through the huge doors, and into the temple auditorium.

One of the pallbearers was none other than Howie Kazanow. The very sight of him made Emily's face red. She could feel it burning. Well, of course he would be here. His wife was the—what did she say she was? recording secretary?—of the Krotonans. She would insist that her hubby put in an appearance at this clambake. And yet it seemed odd. Ardent worshiper of Mammon, Howie was clearly out of place among the Brothers of Light.

In the days when she was still happily married, Emily used to wonder about certain apparently ill-matched couples, speculate on what it might be that kept them together. Now that her own marriage was smashed she realized that she knew nothing of such things. Still, the pairing of Howie and Alma Kazanow struck her as singularly improbable.

Boris Ivanovich Levin was nowhere in sight, not surprising given his feelings toward the deceased, nor was Eddie Green, who was quite likely still looking for a place to park the Cadillac. Nor was Alma Kazanow herself. Howie, when the coffin was safely placed on the Masons' altar, remained with the Krotonans. The mourners as they came streaming in divided into two groups, rather like the bride's and groom's people at a wedding, the movie folks going to the left side and the Krotonans to the right. There was no mistaking the Krotonans. Almost all of them wore odd clothing, like the garments of movie gypsies, and were preternaturally thin. An air hung over them of patchouli and sandalwood. None of them looked like young Englishwomen. Emily wondered where McHenry's daughter was.

The woman who wrote things down stuck with Emily, who still had no idea who she was. She didn't smell like a Theosophist, and her eyes were too small and squinty for the eyes of a movie actress.

And yet she seemed to know Emily. "Aren't you Carl

Laemmle's new director for IMP? You should be over there with the studio people, shouldn't you?"

"I'm sure it doesn't matter," Emily said. An empty seat presented itself. Emily sat in it. To her chagrin the woman sat down right next to her.

"Hester Mink," the woman said, giving her a stiff little handshake. "I think this is so sad, don't you? Did you know the deceased personally?"

"We never met," Emily said. "I admired his work. Most people did. He had a beautiful screen presence."

"Such a fine young man. Such a *fine* young man. I never believed those rumors about the drugs. So sad that he killed himself."

"Er—" Emily was saved from having to reply by a commotion at the back of the auditorium. Hester Mink craned her neck to see the mass of screaming women half in, half out of the huge doors, pushing and struggling against the efforts of the police to eject them. When the doors banged shut, the souls on the outside gave a last despairing groan and the fortunate ones on the inside fell silent.

The spectacle was beginning.

The Masonic altar where the coffin rested was flanked by two immense gold panels, resembling nothing so much as a leftover film set. Emily half expected dancing girls. Instead of girls, a pungent fog of incense rolled from behind the panels, followed by men in robes who took up positions at five-foot intervals and waved palm leaves, their exertions causing the smoke to eddy and swirl. Next came a golden-haired child in a white toga, carrying a brass candlelighter twice as tall as himself. The child solemnly lit the altar candles and paraded out again. The men began to chant in deep, resonant voices.

Then Alma Kazanow glided onto the scene, bedecked in a magnificent headdress and a long cream-colored robe embroidered with glittering jewels and pearls, her hair in a single sandy-colored plait reaching all the way down her back. She took her place behind the altar. In the stillness nothing could be heard but the distant call of a peanut vendor ("Five a bag! They're hot!"). Mrs. Kazanow raised her hands above her head; the full sleeves of the robe fell back to her shoulders, baring her white arms. In a rich, clear voice she pronounced the opening words of the Theosophical funeral rite: "There is but one first cause, uncreated, eternal, infinite, unknown!"

The Theosophists moaned softly.

"Look at that," whispered Hester Mink. "That's the outfit Marguerite Snow wore in *The Buddhist Priestess*."

"Wasn't that a Thanhouser picture?" Emily said.

"What of it?"

"Their studio is in New York. That's a long way for Alma Kazanow to go to raid a wardrobe closet."

"Oh, I expect she had her dressmaker copy it. You say her name is Kazanow? How do you spell that?" Hester Mink was scribbling furiously in her notebook. One of the nearby Krotonans shushed them.

Alma Kazanow continued: "We are gathered here to help our brother Ross on his journey to the next astral plane."

Emily thought privately that McHenry had already had quite enough help in that direction. She gazed around the auditorium, wondering which if any among the umpty thousand had given brother Ross the push. There sat Marilyn Slater, McHenry's ravishing blond costar, dabbing her eyes with a lace handkerchief. Would she have had reason to kill him? Only if one believed the story that they were lovers. Lovers can always find a reason to kill the thing they love. Adam's face drifted unbidden across her mind's eye, and Emily turned her attention to Uncle Carl Laemmle.

The powerful mogul was certainly eager enough to hush the story up. What if he killed McHenry himself? He was frowning, but not in a grief-stricken way, rather in the way he might frown if he were deeply concerned over the future of *Dark Star of India* and the finances of IMP. But suppose McHenry had meant to quit the picture. Laemmle, in a rage . . . oh, no. Not that kindly, avuncular figure. And surely not in McHenry's bedroom, while he was dressed in nothing but a blue damask robe.

Snuggled up to Uncle Carl sat Babette de Long, sobbing, her shoulders shaking. Her mother—yes! It was the very same woman, the one called Mrs. Swaine, all swathed in black—put her arm around her. Little Babs pulled away with a snarl. Both women were weeping now. The sound of it was drowned in the weeping of the crowd, most of them people who knew Ross McHenry only from his films.

"Did you see my column today?"

"Oh, do you write a column?" Emily said.

"I haven't made up my mind whether I actually got it right. What do *you* think? Did Ross McHenry kill himself? Or do you suppose he might have been, oh, I don't know, murdered? Perhaps Babette de Long killed him."

"Good heavens! I certainly hope not," Emily said.

"That's right, you wouldn't want Little Babs to be hanged for murder, would you, Miss Daggett? You need her. She's the only reason Carl Laemmle wants to make *Captain Jinks* at all. Without Little Babs"—the detestable woman actually giggled—"you'd have no picture to direct." Emily's horror must have registered on her face. "I'm sorry. Didn't you know that?"

"Shush," the woman behind them said.

Yes, Emily thought, shush, in the name of the one first cause, uncreated, infinite, unknown. The picture was for Babs? How did this woman come to know all of Emily's business, anyway? Why didn't someone else tell her these things before she was ambushed by evil reporters?

Fortunately, Hester Mink had the good taste to shush for the rest of the service, so that Emily was not forced to succumb to the temptation to slap her. At last Alma Kazanow uttered the final Theosophical blessing, "In the sure and certain hope that our brother will join us again soon." She spread her arms wide and gazed down the center aisle. Heads turned, as if people expected Ross McHenry to come strolling cheerfully down the aisle, maybe doing a few of his famous handsprings.

Little Babs seemed to be struggling to her feet. She was terribly pale; the whites of her eyes showed all around the irises.

Hester Mink snickered. "Join us soon? I believe the traffic is usually in the other direction."

"The Theosophists believe in reincarnation," Emily said.

"Oh, really? I thought all they believed in was closing the saloons to keep me from getting a drink."

"There's a lot more to it than that."

"So you think the dead return in new bodies?"

"I? No, but the Theosophists claim to think so."

"Interesting. By the way, you're from the East, aren't you, Miss Daggett? Fort Lee, isn't it? Did you know Agnes Gelert when you were there? Such a charming girl. I understand she's the up-and-coming new—"

Emily felt like screaming. Instead it was Marilyn Slater who screamed, a fortunate interruption for Emily. The grieving blonde sprang from her seat and hurtled up the aisle.

"Ah, poor girl," Hester Mink said. "He killed himself for love of her. Or did he? I'm not quite certain yet. Watch this, it ought to be good."

And it was good; Emily had enjoyed the scene the first time she saw it, in *The Young Widow's Grief* from Biograph Studios in 1910. Black dress billowing, hands balled into despairing fists (an acting technique favored by Biograph director D. W. Griffith), locks of blond hair escaping wildly from under her severe black hat, Marilyn Slater threw herself on the coffin and fainted.

ELEVEN

Miss Slater's performance at Ross McHenry's funeral was so spectacular that it completely masked the quiet collapse of Little Babs. By the time the spectators took their eyes off the blonde's histrionics, the rest of the studio people had left the auditorium. It wasn't until the following day that Emily learned from Holbert Bruns that Babs had been packed off to Glendale Sanitarium.

They were breakfasting at the studio commissary, where there were fresh oranges and better coffee than what could be had at the Hotel Hollywood. Bruns had read Emily's typed report without comment. Her life in Hollywood was settling into a rhythm, the breakfast meeting with Bruns, the after-breakfast meeting with Carl Laemmle, lunch at the commissary, then the wild afternoon of unfettered detecting. The clues they had gathered in McHenry's house were spread before them on the oilcloth table covering, but before addressing these items they were addressing their food.

Emily buttered her toast. "How badly off is Little Babs, anyway?"

"They're keeping her confined in the mental ward."

"What did she do to get herself locked up?"

"Something involving her mother's face and a sharp instrument. I didn't inquire too deeply."

"She's in a straitjacket?"

"I'm fairly certain."

"A shame. There goes my picture. Hester Mink told me at the funeral that Carl Laemmle was making *Captain Jinks* solely as a vehicle for Babs. No Babs, no picture." No jam, either. Emily ate the last of her toast and considered going back for an egg.

"Good Lord. You were talking to Hester Mink? What did you tell her?"

"Nothing. I don't talk to newspaper people. What do you take me for?"

"What did she tell *you*, then?"

"In spite of the column you got her to write she says she hasn't made up her mind yet whether McHenry killed himself or was murdered."

"She used the word 'murdered.'"

"Yes."

"She have any ideas about who did the murdering?"

"Not that she said."

"What about McHenry's daughter? Did you see anything of her?"

"No."

Holbert Bruns finished his coffee. He took the stack of snapshots in his elegant square hands and dealt them out on the table one by one. Sepia-tone views of fun on a beach, taken with a Brownie camera; beyond the beach, a flight of steps, the risers inlaid with curiously decorated tiles.

Here was Ross McHenry in a bathing costume, grinning into the sun and holding a huge beach ball. What a handsome man. What a waste his death was. Another angle showed the same tiled steps leading up to a house, Spanish in feeling but modern, almost hidden in tropical foliage.

The other snapshots were similar, shots of McHenry posing and clowning, taken on that very beach, in front of that very beach house. No one else was in any of the pictures, although Emily could see someone's shadow in one of them; she made out a wide-brimmed hat.

"There's your killer," Holbert Bruns said. "Boris, in one of those hats the Theosophists wear."

"No, it's a woman," Emily said. "In a skirt, don't you see?"

"A trick of the light."

"It's a woman. Her lip rouge is on these pencil stubs." She held one of them up, greasy red, dented with the prints of molars.

"Not necessarily the spoor of the beach photographer."

"But the lip rouge at least proves that McHenry played cards with women."

"Does it?"

"Yes. That was McHenry's card drawer. He kept his playing cards and poker chips there. And also these slips of paper. The letters and numbers are the initials of people he played cards with and their scores, don't you see?"

"Maybe he wore lip rouge himself. Or it came from your friend Boris. Wait a minute. Whose initials—?"

Emily examined the score sheets. "R—that would be Ross McHenry—played cards against A sometimes, H sometimes, and sometimes B. Hmm. B always lost."

"Boris?"

"Babs, I'm guessing. Boris is too intelligent to lose all the time." They stared at the little pile of clues. Emily could almost hear Bruns's mind working. "So what shall we tell Mr. Laemmle this morning?" she said at last.

"That we are proceeding with our inquiries."

"Okay. Right," Emily said. "And specifically, that we have cleared McHenry's house of everything that might make him or the studio look bad, except of course for the fatal bloodstains, and that McHenry's daughter, whoever she might be, arranged for the Theosophists to bury him, or possibly cremate his remains, for whatever reason. Also that McHenry's body was dressed in a blue damask robe when it was found, and also—"

"I'm not sure he wants that level of detail. Tell you what," Bruns said. "I'll talk to Mr. Laemmle this morning."

"Without me?"

"It'll be all right."

"Be sure and remind him that Boris is coming for his screen test."

"Today?"

"Any minute."

Holbert Bruns muttered something that Emily didn't quite catch and went to keep the morning appointment with Laemmle. Emily scooped up the collection of clues, thrust them back in her handbag, and looked around to see if there was anything for her to detect.

At another oilcloth-covered corner table over by the door Marilyn Slater was having coffee and eggs, in full makeup for *Dark Star of India*. Her radiant hair was hidden under a black wig. Evidently the studio was still shooting around Ross McHenry's part in the hope that he could be replaced, which meant that Boris still had a chance. Good.

Miss Slater's face was altogether free of the ravages of grief; nonetheless Emily felt compelled to extend her sympathies. "I'm so sorry for your loss, Miss Slater."

"Thanks, sweetie, but I haven't lost anything yet." The actress brushed a loose strand of false hair out of her face, took out a cigarette and lit up, blowing the smoke out through her nose. There was no trace of a Louisiana plantation in her speech. Hackensack, New Jersey, Emily would have guessed, deepened by years of whiskey and tobacco. "With any luck Laemmle will have another male lead for the picture by the end of the week."

"I meant, the loss of Mr. McHenry. I understood that you two were—"

"Oh, him. No, nothing was really going on there. He liked—well, not me. We weren't each other's type. The romance was pure studio publicity."

"But you fainted on his coffin."

"I need some ink, honey. I have to keep my face in front of the public. If *Dark Star of India* goes down the drain my movie career goes with it. You know how it is. Say, who's that handsome devil?"

In the doorway stood Boris, looking around for Emily. Under the traditional Theosophist broad-brimmed black hat he wore the sort of shirt an Indian prince might wear, white silk with gaudy embroidery; possibly this, too, was a Theosophist uniform of some kind. Emily approved. Having a colorful wardrobe of one's own was a distinct asset in pictures.

She waved to him. "That's Boris Levin. He's here to take a screen test for the lead in your picture. May we sit with you for a minute?"

"Feel free." Miss Slater scooted her chair over to make sure there was plenty of room right next to her.

Emily introduced them; Boris bent and kissed Miss Slater's hand. She put out her cigarette, made an effort to look maidenly, and invited him to sit. Emily went to the cafeteria line and fetched the actor a glass of tea and a sweet roll to fortify him against the stresses of the coming screen test.

When she returned to the table Boris was deep in a disquisition on his philosophy of the art of moving pictures. "In theater the actor reacts to events and feels emotion, thereby calling forth sympathetic emotion from audience. In cinema, events speak to audience directly. You see an event and have feelings yourself in reaction. You are seeing difference?"

"That's sweet, honey," Miss Slater said. "And here I thought there was nothing to making movies but money and sex."

"Money is good to have," Boris said. "Sex also. But, art! Art is immortal."

"I'll drink to that. Get me some, too, will you, sweetie?"

"It's tea," Emily said.

"That's okay," Miss Slater said. "I'll drink it anyway."

"Take mine," Boris said, sparing Emily the necessity of making a scene over being asked to fetch tea. "I am unable to partake before performing."

"I understand," Miss Slater said, squeezing his free hand. When she took the tea in her right hand he covered her left hand with his own. So intimate. To see them together you would have thought their two souls were twining together as one. All the while Miss Slater gulped down the glass of tea her rapt gaze never left Boris's face. But they were actors. Marilyn Slater's career depended on the studio's hiring a leading man before the money dried up for *Dark Star of India*. Boris Levin's future depended on his getting the part, which for all he knew depended on Miss Slater's approval.

He raised her hand to his lips and murmured something. She kissed him lightly, said she had to get back to the set, and left, smiling. It was a stunning performance. Or they really liked each other. No telling which.

"Boris, did you ever see Miss Slater before?"

"In the cinema."

"Did you ever see her with Ross McHenry?"

"Only in the cinema."

"She never visited his house?"

He shook his head. "No. Why?"

"I was hoping you might be able to tell me who Mr. McHenry's friends were, the people who came to see him. Maybe he had, I don't know, parties."

"Mr. McHenry did not give parties. But people came and went in his house."

"What people?"

"The ladies of Krotona. All the time."

"Mrs. Kazanow?"

"And others. They have monthly meetings. They hold Mr. McHenry in high regard. They think he is one of them."

"He wasn't one of them?"

"He eats steaks when they aren't around. He drinks whiskey. No. He wasn't."

"But they gave him a big funeral."

"Very strange. I think so myself."

"Why would he pretend to be a Theosophist?"

"Is real estate deal. He wanted the house."

"Don't tell me they gave him that lovely little house."

"They sold him the house. The house is part of Krotona community. You must belong to buy the house."

"But if he held monthly meetings—!"

Boris took out a Fatima cigarette, rank and stinky with Turkish tobacco, put it between his lips, and held a match to it. "Ross McHenry is rotten bastard. I told you that already." He puffed. The oval end of the cigarette glowed red. "What he likes—what he liked—was to fool people.

Ladies came to his house every month, he talked to them, and he fooled them. When they left he had a big laugh."

"Are you saying he despised them?"

"That is word. Despised." He blew out a long stream of smoke.

"Who else was in his life?"

"For instance what?"

"His other friends."

"Ah, well. Some so-called friends he despised all night long. Mrs. Kazanow, for one, when Mr. Kazanow was out of town."

"Good heavens."

"And that one." He waved his reeking cigarette in the direction of the door. Mrs. Swaine had just walked in, still limping, still all swathed in black, a deeply bereaved woman. "Her. Also the daughter. Only at different times. Never together."

"The daughter?" Emily said, lowering her voice as Mrs. Swaine passed by on her way to the food counter. "You mean Mr. McHenry's daughter?"

"That one's daughter. The little actress. Maybe he really liked some of them. Is no telling with rotten bastards. Then there was a certain man, every Friday night—my night off, Friday—"

"I've heard rumors about men. May I ask you something?"

"Ask all you like."

"What were you doing the night of April twenty-fourth?"

"I was in whorehouse, with twelve witnesses. If you like I give you names."

"Oh, my. Well, tell me this, then. Did Ross McHenry ever make a pass at you?"

He drew himself up until he was looking down his nose at her; his eyes flashed fire. Oh, dear, she thought, I've offended him. Only Holbert Bruns could get away with asking questions like that. People expected him to be blunt.

"Of *course* Ross McHenry made pass at me. Everyone makes pass at me. I cannot understand why *you* have never made pass at me. But Boris Ivanovich Levin is not inclined that way, to entertain passes from other men. Women, yes." He put his hand on her knee. "Perhaps you wish to make pass at me now."

"No, Boris." She took his hand away. "Thanks anyhow. Are you ready for your screen test, or would you like something else to eat first?" The sweet roll sat on his plate untouched. She thought of eating it herself, but it didn't look appetizing. Since Adam's departure hardly anything did.

"Nothing here is fit to eat. Pfui." He crushed the cigarette on the sole of his boot and threw it on the linoleum floor. "Boris Ivanovich Levin performs on an empty stomach. Be showing me to dressing room."

In the hall they found out from one of Carl Laemmle's nephews where the dressing room was that had been reserved for Boris. Emily, still curious about the life and times of Ross McHenry, followed him in. Boris blithely stripped down to his union suit and began to apply greasepaint from a kit he had brought with him. His lack of decorous clothing was all the same to Emily; they were both actors, after all. As he patted, smoothed, penciled, and powdered, she pumped him for information about McHenry. He rewarded her with a catalogue of the film star's habits.

Once a month McHenry hobnobbed with the women of Krotona. Every Wednesday evening he had a social engagement with friends in town. (Could that have been bathhouse night?) Three times a week he exercised at the Los Angeles Athletic Club. Every evening at six o'clock he became noticeably ill, unless he was able to retire to his bedroom and restore himself.

"How do you mean, noticeably ill?"

"Pale; shaky; vomiting."

"Good heavens."

"Perhaps it was his heart. There was medicine he took."

The hypodermic syringe. The tablets. "I see. So, tell me, what are you going to do now that he's gone?"

"Firstly I find someplace else to live," Boris said, brushing the loose powder off his face with a rabbit's foot. "If I get a part in this movie I can do that more easily, I think." He reached for the trousers of his rajah costume. "Landlords prefer their tenants to have the regular income."

"I hope you get the part," she said. "But to get back to the man who visited him on Fridays. Have you any idea who that might have—?"

The door burst open; on the threshold stood Holbert Bruns. Suddenly Emily was embarrassed to be seen alone with Boris in his underwear. Ridiculous, no? And yet here was Bruns glaring at her like a jealous lover. In the doorway behind Holbert Bruns stood Carl Laemmle's nephew, calling to Boris that they were ready for him.

Ignoring Bruns, Boris got into his wardrobe tunic, did up his pants, and fastened the jeweled belt around himself. He took a last glance in the mirror. What he saw seemed to please him.

"I know you'll be great," Emily said. She patted his shoulder.

"Yes," Boris said. "I am great. But will they recognize my greatness?" Away he went with the nephew, to stand or fall by his merits.

As soon as Boris was out of sight an icy chill settled over the dressing room. Bruns sat down in front of the makeup mirror and began to poke in Boris's kit. "I hope you realize, Miss Daggett, that you've talked Mr. Laemmle into hiring Ross McHenry's murderer to take his place in the movie." He took out a stick of greasepaint and sniffed it. "I don't know how you feel about that, but to me it seems unjust."

That Holbert Bruns would consider the concept of justice seemed strange to Emily. Weren't they trying to solve the case in order to let the murderer go free, for the good of the studio? Where was the justice in that? Something else was troubling Bruns, surely not injustice. "Boris Levin had no reason to murder Ross McHenry. It's not as though he had any idea he might get McHenry's part in this picture." It was true that Boris had seemed quite cross at Mr. McHenry, and had gone so far as to call him a rotten bastard two or three times in Emily's hearing. Still, it seemed to her unlikely that he would do that if he had already taken the man's life.

Bruns put the greasepaint back in the kit and picked up the metal tray that held it. What did he expect to find underneath? The murder weapon? A written confession? "Miss Daggett, your new star is a murderous Bolshevik fruit. He and McHenry were lovers. Of course he killed him."

"I don't follow your logic, Mr. Bruns. Besides, it was my understanding from things Mr. Levin said to me that Mr. McHenry never enjoyed his favors. To me it seems far more likely that the mystery man who came to see him every Friday night is the guilty party."

"What mystery man?"

"Boris says he met some man every Friday, when Boris had the night off."

"Boris says. Of course we take his word for it, this person with whom you are inordinately, I might say, indecently, friendly."

"What are you talking about?"

"Well, what am I to think? I come in here and the man is putting his clothes back on."

Emily sighed. "Mr. Bruns, I know you are a person of enormous worldliness and sophistication, but you're not familiar with the habits of stage folks. Naked, clothed, it's all the same to us. Our bodies are mere instruments."

He put a handful of brushes back in the makeup kit and closed it with a bang. "I'm learning fast. You people are as loony as those Theosophists." Boris's broad-brimmed hat attracted his attention next. He poked under the hatband, his nose wrinkled with distaste. "I must confess I'm at a loss to understand what you see in this fellow."

"I don't see anything in him. I certainly don't see him murdering his employer."

"Why are you so determined to defend him?"

"He's an actor. I like actors, even though they tend to be—"

"Defective human beings."

"I was going to say, unconscious of what's really going on around them. They wrap themselves up in fantasies. I've never known a real actor to kill anyone."

"And you are certainly a woman of broad experience."

"I talk to Boris because Boris knows a lot about Ross McHenry. In his dizzy way he seems to have kept a close eye on him. He told me a great deal about his habits."

"You like him as a source. I can understand that. But why do you want him working for Carl Laemmle?"

Could Bruns have forgotten that Emily came to Hollywood to direct moving pictures? Patiently, she explained: "If Boris doesn't take over Ross McHenry's role in *Dark Star of India,* Mr. Laemmle may never finish the picture, and the studio may never go on to make *Captain Jinks of the Horse Marines*. If that happens I'll have no movie to direct. I need *Jinks*."

"What for?"

"For one thing, I just hired four actresses for it. If they don't get the work, they'll starve."

"You really want to direct pictures."

"Well, yes."

So there he sat, staring at the toes of his boots, evidently trying to understand why Emily would want to be anything other than a detective, until Boris came back from his screen test and began to peel off his Indian prince costume. Then Bruns shifted his gaze to Emily and raised his eyebrows expectantly. What could she do? She left the room. It was the only decent thing.

TWELVE

The screen test was sufficiently successful for Mr. Laemmle to offer Boris a contract on the strength of it. With *Dark Star of India* proceeding on schedule Emily dared to hope that the studio would soon be ready to film *Captain Jinks of the Horse Marines.*

Holbert Bruns was still unhappy with this arrangement when Mr. Laemmle told him of it at their regular morning meeting. "Before you sign Boris Levin to a contract, there's something you may want to consider, Mr. Laemmle," he said. "Levin might have murdered Ross McHenry."

"Is there any evidence of this?"

"He was working as McHenry's yard boy; he makes no secret of the fact that he hated him; naturally—"

"Not naturally. What you say is nonsense, Mr. Bruns. I

am not paying you to spout nonsense. The talent of Boris Levin is essential to finishing *Dark Star of India*. Because we have him, we will save close to a million dollars in losses. How can he be guilty of murder? It's not possible."

"But motive, opportunity, everything points—"

"Furthermore Marilyn Slater has expressed a great fondness for this man. A studio romance. The box office potential is stupendous."

"Can I hire some actresses for *Jinks* now?" Emily said, stepping forward. "These girls are lovely, clever young persons with experience in the stage production. They need money right away." In fact they were waiting in the commissary.

"No. Not until *Dark Star of India* is finished and the scandal with McHenry dies down."

"But that could be—"

"It is way too soon to hire actresses."

"But—"

"I'll tell you what you can do, Miss Daggett, to hasten this process. You can go out to the Glendale Sanitarium this afternoon and see Miss de Long. Woman to woman. Tell her about the picture."

"So we're actually waiting for her to recover? Wouldn't it make more sense to hire another—"

"No, no. Our Little Babs can handle it. She'll be up and around in no time at all. Get Eddie to drive you out to Glendale this afternoon. I'll call the sanitarium and tell them you're coming. Give her a nice pep talk. Cheer her up. Tell her the part is waiting for her. Tell her to get well soon."

"Yes, sir." Emily doubted that anything she would be able to deliver in the way of a pep talk would have much effect on the girl, not if she were as badly off as Bruns thought. Still, she would at least get to talk to her. Ever since Flagstaff she had wanted to talk to her. Or listen to her. Some story worth hearing was behind those haunted eyes.

"And no more from either one of you about murder. Ross McHenry was not murdered."

"Yes, sir," they said.

The girls still waited in the commissary, looking hungry, goggling at all the film stars, and twittering among themselves.

"Did you see that, Etta? It was King Baggot."

"He winked at you, Wanda."

"He never. Did he?"

"Are these your actresses?" Holbert Bruns said.

"They're really extremely steady girls."

"You'd better tell them, then."

Emily made introductions: "Etta Sweet, Wanda Rose, Gertrude Canty, this is Holbert Bruns, my boss."

"Not Baby Wanda Rose?" Bruns said.

"Tell us what?" Gertrude said.

"Do I look like a baby to you?" Wanda said.

"Tell us what?" Gertrude repeated.

"Mr. Laemmle won't let you have screen tests yet," Emily said. "Production of *Jinks* has been postponed."

"Well, darn. What are we going to do for lunch?"

Gertrude said. "They won't feed us at the boardinghouse until suppertime."

"You're staying in a boardinghouse now?" Emily said.

"You know Millie, Mr. Laemmle's receptionist? She got her landlady to rent us a room," Wanda said.

"It's quite nice," Etta said. "If a bit small for the three of us."

"We told the old lady we were going to get paid today," Wanda said. "I guess we lied."

Emily took Bruns aside. "You once told me a woman could go places you couldn't go," she said.

"True."

"Three women can go three places you can't go."

"I can't argue with that, Miss Daggett." He stared at the actresses, rubbing his chin, pursing his lips. "Are you ladies sober and industrious?" he said finally.

Gertrude spoke up. "If it will get us lunch."

"Mr. Bruns is going to buy you lunch. Isn't that so, Mr. Bruns? And then he's going to put you on the payroll as confidential operatives."

Etta was outraged. "Oh, no, you don't. If I wanted that kind of life I could have stayed in Flagstaff with the cowboys."

"No, no. Nothing like that. We're investigating a murder. Don't mention it to a soul. You're all going to be detectives now, the Vine Street Irregulars." Etta and Wanda exchanged suspicious glances. "It's a literary allusion," Emily said.

Bruns insisted on a training session before he would call them his employees. "You, too, Miss Daggett. You're

carrying around a gun that you don't know how to shoot."
He took them to the IMP back lot, a scruffy, weed-grown
yard, where he made them all fire at a tomato can he set up
on a pile of hay bales.

Emily, the first to try, used Billie Burke's little pearl-
handled five-shooter with the disappearing trigger. Even
though she had only the vaguest idea of how it worked, she
felt a curious intimacy with the thing. She was expecting
the recoil, having shot a gun once before—the time she
blasted Grogan in the foot—but she was surprised at how
easy it was to aim it using the gun sight. Hitting a tomato
can dead center was effortless, even at forty feet; she simply thought of Adam and drew a bead. Sometimes she
imagined Agnes Gelert's face. Too bad there were only five
shots.

The other girls took their turns, using the Browning
automatic that Bruns kept holstered against his chest.
Whether it was her particular firearm or some innate skill
she had, Emily proved to be the best shot of all of them.
After the shooting was over Bruns showed her how to clean
her gun safely and gave her a new box of ammunition.

"Where'd you get that?"

"Had it around. Thirty-two caliber rimfire, same as
mine."

He kept a set of lock picks in his jacket pocket. They
took turns using it on the back door of the studio. Gertrude learned the lock picks faster than any of them, so
fast that Emily had a moment of wondering what she used
to do for a living before she became an actress. The others
weren't bad either, with their dexterous little hands, nor

was Emily when her turn came, though none of the women was as quick as Bruns at popping the lock open.

Etta was the last to finish; she was perspiring profusely. "Do we get certificates now?"

"You won't need them," Bruns said. "You'll be real detectives when you can keep your eyes and ears open, lie like rugs, and run like thieves. That's all you need."

"When do we get paid?" Gertrude said.

"Right now." He gave them each five dollars, an awful lot of money.

"And what do we have to do for this?" Gertrude said.

"Get on the Vine Street Red Car and go up to Krotona. Miss Daggett can't do that anymore; they know her."

"To look for what?" Gertrude said.

"Ross McHenry's killer. But keep quiet about it."

Etta shook her head. "I thought they said he—"

"As far as the public knows his death was an accident. Mr. Laemmle wants them to continue to believe this. But Ross McHenry was gunned down in his bedroom, probably on the night of April twenty-fourth, by a person or persons unknown."

"Well, but how can we—"

"I want you to go up to the street where he lived and talk to his neighbors. Find out whether anyone saw or heard anything suspicious that night. Or at any other time. But don't tip them off about the murder. You're smart girls. Go on up there and be clever. And be careful. Anyone you talk to could be a killer."

"Don't we need guns, then?" Etta said.

"I shouldn't think so. Stay where people can see you. If

you don't look threatening you should be fine." He told them the address of McHenry's house on Temple Hill Drive.

"No guns," Etta said, crestfallen, as the Irregulars filed out the door.

His new assistants gone, Holbert Bruns stared thoughtfully at Emily. Clearly it was time for her to leave, but before she could make her escape Bruns sat down on the hay bale, pushing the battered tomato can aside, and patted the spot next to himself. "Have a seat, Miss Daggett. You and your actress friends did very well today."

"Thank you," she said, and settled her bottom on the prickly hay.

"Very well indeed. You particularly. I never would have figured you for a markswoman."

"Must be the pistol," she said. "It feels very . . . I don't know . . . friendly in my hand."

"You can make better friends than that." He took out his pipe and performed his slow ritual of lighting it, putting the match out with care so as not to set the hay on fire. "I don't know whether I've told you how pleased I am to have you working with me on this case. A girl of your intelligence and nerve can have any sort of life she wants here in California. I hope you're aware of that."

"The life I want is in pictures. I can have that in California or back east in New Jersey, the way I used to."

"You might reconsider," he said. "The future of the private investigation business is wide open in Los Angeles. There's no limit to what an energetic detective agency can achieve here."

"The Energetic Detective Agency," Emily said. "Has a nice ring to it."

"Quite seriously, Miss Daggett, it appears that I now have four operatives working for me, thanks to you, and even though they're all women I think it's a good beginning."

"But what we all really want to do is to work in moving pictures."

"You might not succeed in pictures. Sometimes people don't. In case things don't work out— Gertrude is a smart girl, don't you think?"

"Gertrude is a stunning beauty and a clever actress. If she isn't a star in six months' time I'll be surprised."

"She was good with the lock picks."

"If you're looking for help in the detective business, Mr. Bruns, Etta is your woman. That's my opinion, anyway. She notices things, and she shoots pretty well, too, as I'm sure you'll agree."

"But not you."

"All I want to do is direct moving pictures."

"Why?"

How to explain to a detective a desire to make art? "When you're on a case, you have a mystery to solve, isn't that so? You have a group of people to work with, and your work is to discover what's in their hearts. Some will be innocent, some guilty. You find out the truth."

"I suppose that's the way it is, yes."

"When I'm on a picture, the important thing is what's in *my* heart. I already have the truth of things, artistically speaking, and my work is to use the actors, the camera-men, the sets, and the lighting to make images on the screen that will convey this truth to an audience."

"I see. You're not happy unless you're the boss."

"Maybe that's it."

"It's a very masculine view of life."

"Be that as it may, it's my view."

"But you do so well adapting to uncertain circum-stances and threats of danger. No, I mean it, Miss Daggett. This is an unusual quality in a woman. Sometimes I think you're the most valuable assistant I've ever had." He took a puff of his pipe. "I'll miss you when this case is all cleared up and you go off to be a director."

"Well, thank you." That old feeling of magnetism was rolling off him again. They were sitting too close. Some-thing told her it would be good to kiss him now. She said to herself, No it wouldn't, it would be ill-timed, problem-atical, and ultimately ruinous. She gathered her hat and handbag.

"In any case I hope you'll consider my offer. I'm willing to give you all the autonomy you want. Personal and pro-fessional. Personal and professional."

What? What offer? "It's time for me to go and see Babs."

"This is the sort of thing I mean. I could never get close to that girl. While you, a woman—and with your sympa-thy and warmth—"

"I'm going to look for Eddie now. He's supposed to drive me."

"Yes. Eddie. While you're at it, see if you can find out what he knows," Bruns said. "Engage him in conversation."

"Eddie knows things?"

"He knows a lot about the seamy side of Los Angeles. He might have heard what really happened to Ross McHenry. While you're at it, find out what he was doing the night of the murder. But don't let him give you any pills or powders, and don't go down any dark alleys with him. Remember, he's not one of your harmless actors. Chicago Eddie Green is a dangerous man."

THIRTEEN

Eddie Green was perfectly willing to let Emily engage him in conversation. He invited her to sit up front with him in the Cadillac during the drive to Glendale and gave her a driving lesson as well. First he showed her how to start the car. "Even a girl can do it. It's the electric starter, see." Then, between handy tips on how to shift gears and when to weave in and out of traffic (you watched the car in front of the car in front of you, he said), he proceeded to deliver a steady stream of travelogue: here was so-and-so's ranch, there was such-and-such an orange farm, this was a good place to turn off the road and park, you could see almost clear to Mexico. Emily declined to turn off the road and park. She wanted to get Eddie talking about the night Ross McHenry was killed, not to invite his amorous attentions.

"I was so sorry not to be at home on the twenty-fourth of April," she said. "I mean, in New York. It was my birthday."

"You got someone special there?"

"Well, I used to have. We had birthday traditions. What do you do on your birthday? Or what did you do on *my* birthday? The twenty-fourth of April? It was a Friday." Maybe he would say, I murdered Ross McHenry. Or, I drove some people from the studio to his house so they could murder him. That would clear everything up, and then she could start filming *Jinks*.

"Did what I always do," he said, grinning, exhibiting the dimples again. "I made people happy."

"That must be nice."

"You think all I do is drive folks around. I'm a lot more important than that. To the studio."

"I'm sure. Why, you're—"

"No, I mean it. They couldn't get nothing done without me. Without what I give 'em. How do you think all them stars get up in front of a camera sixteen hours a day? They wasn't born with that kind of stamina."

"Pills and powders?"

He smirked at her. "Okay, sweetheart, here it is." But instead of offering her drugs he stopped the car in front of the Glendale Sanitarium, an imposing pile with a veranda, festooned with cupolas, balconies, and chimneys, and surmounted by a pointed tower. Emily's New England eye told her that the chimneys would never draw, being lower than the cupola and the tower, but this was Southern California, after all, and the inmates probably didn't need the heat. The lawn was lush and green, the flower beds neatly kept. Pleasant and welcoming. No fence. Maybe their patients weren't all that crazy.

"Can you wait for me, Eddie? I won't be very long."

"Sugar, for you I'll wait all day."

Inside the front door happy patients strolled arm in arm, glowing. Glendale Sanitarium was a well-known resort, a mission of the Seventh-Day Adventists, part of a nationwide chain where the sick and weary could experience renewed health through the most modern methods of diet, exercise, and rest. A flowery statement of their mission was framed and posted behind the receptionist's desk. It almost made Emily want to stay there.

The receptionist called an attendant, big and ugly enough to be the bouncer at a downtown saloon, to escort Emily to the severely disabled wing to see Babette de Long. Behind the locked door to that wing of the sanitarium, life appeared to be somewhat less rosy. From the farther corridors came screams that might have been the howls of the damned. Emily's hackles began to stir.

A door burst open and a gaunt person in striped pajamas lunged at her, his eyes ringed with purple. He held her by the shoulders. "Can you take me out of this place? I want to go home, and I can't find my truck." He smelled faintly of feces.

"Go back to your room, Dennis," the attendant said. "Don't annoy the visitors." He put a beefy hand on Dennis's upper arm and propelled him back through the door. "There you go, now." The door swung to with a click. The attendant tested it, jerking on the knob. Finding the seal satisfactory, he continued onward.

A little old woman pattered past them in carpet slippers, wringing her hands and muttering, "Not the yogurt again . . . please . . . not the yogurt . . ." More shouts; more doors banging. The attendant stopped in front of a thick oak door.

"This is Miss de Long's room," he said. He unlocked it with one of the keys that hung from his belt. Noticing Emily's face, he added, "We only lock it to keep the rest of the patients out. You know how it is . . . Miss de Long! Feeling better today? I brought you a visitor."

Babette de Long lay motionless, facing the wall, in her hygienic, white-painted iron bed. She wore a hospital nightgown but not a straitjacket. Her room was severely plain, painted a pale lavender, a color known to soothe the agitated. It wasn't padded, exactly, but there was nothing in it that a distraught person could use to hurt himself, or to hurt the staff; nothing sharp, nothing heavy and blunt, nothing that might be used as a ligature, except perhaps for the nightgown and bedsheets. One could always tear up nightgowns or bedsheets and hang oneself on the doorknob. There was, however, no doorknob on the inside. The attendant stepped outside and closed the door.

Emily fought down a surge of panic and gave her attention to the patient. "Miss de Long?"

The girl rolled over and sat up. "Who are you?"

"I'm Emily Daggett, from the studio."

"I thought it was my mother again. I can't get her to leave me alone. Do you have a cigarette?"

"No, I'm sorry, I don't smoke."

"They won't let me have cigarettes. Do you have a

drink? I need a drink. They won't let me drink either. All they let me have is yogurt enemas."

"Perhaps I can get you some fruit juice." Seeing the look on the girl's face, Emily added, "To drink."

"I don't want fruit juice. Why did you come here?"

"Mr. Laemmle sent me. I'm going to be directing *Captain Jinks of the Horse Marines*. He wants—we all want you to get well quickly so that we can start work."

"Don't want to work. If my mother would let me have all the money I've already made I would never have to work again."

"What do you want to do with your life?"

"Nothing. I want to die."

"You won't need money for that."

"Get me a drink. Is Eddie outside? Ask him to get me something."

"No."

"No?"

"No."

"People don't say no to me."

"I do."

"Who the hell are you?"

"I am the woman who says no to you. I am the woman who wants you to get better so that we can make a movie together. *Captain Jinks of the Horse Marines*. Remember that? I would like to start filming as soon as possible."

"Go to hell."

"Miss de Long, I can see that something is troubling you. Perhaps you would like to talk about it."

"It doesn't matter. Nothing matters."

Two short raps on the handleless door and a smartly uniformed nurse came in carrying a spatterware pitcher of ice water and a tin cup. "You should leave now," she murmured to Emily. "Miss de Long can't stand much excitement." She put the water and cup down on the table beside the bed.

"What's wrong with her?" Emily whispered.

"Stop talking about me."

"Acute melancholia."

"Can you tell me how long before she—"

"I can hear you, you know."

"You really should go," the nurse said.

"Give me five more minutes. I promise not to say anything exciting."

"I'm going to send the attendant to show you the way out." The nurse closed the door behind herself, maybe thinking that Emily might go out in the hall and stir up the other patients.

Better make this quick. "Tell me about Ross McHenry."

"He's dead."

"Yes."

"My mother killed him. My mother kills everything I love."

"Why do you say that?"

"She hated him. She said he ruined her life. She couldn't stay away from him. When she saw him in the movie theater she had to come to Hollywood and find him. She used me."

"She saw him in the movie theater?"

"On the screen. In a picture. She said to me, 'My God,

Barbara, that's your father.' We were in Toronto. I was supposed to be playing in *Peter Pan* that night."

"You're Ross McHenry's daughter?" That would fit; the Canadians were British subjects, with British passports.

"She always used to tell me he was dead."

"Here. Drink this." Emily held the glass of water up to the girl's mouth and she gulped it down.

"We came to Hollywood and looked him up." She wiped her mouth on the back of her arm. "Turns out he didn't want anyone to know. His career depended on people thinking he was younger. I went to visit him secretly." She finished the glass of water.

"Not so secretly as all that."

"What do you mean?"

"There were people who noticed."

"My mother was after him all the time."

"I guess there were people who noticed that, too."

The girl's face crumpled; she began to weep and hit her head on the rail of the iron bed. "She killed him. She killed him, she killed him, he didn't want her and she killed him."

"Here, stop that. You'll hurt yourself." Emily pulled the girl away from the bed rail. "Calm down." She held her by her thin shoulders and dabbed at her forehead with a cold, wet cloth. Was this what detecting meant, soothing the agitated, interrogating the distraught? She could have chosen to be a nurse, the way her mother wanted her to. There would have been more future in it. But Emily herself had never wanted to be a nurse; the sight of sick people upset her. At that very moment pity for this demented girl was choking her until she could scarcely breathe.

Babette de Long sobbed, gulped, wiped her nose on the sleeve of her nightgown, and looked into Emily's face with enormous blue eyes. "Don't tell anyone. She's my mother. They mustn't hang her."

"How do you know she killed him?"

"She shot him. We had to carry the body away."

"You and your mother carried the body away?"

"We beat his head with rocks, again and again, so no one would see the bullet holes. Then we threw him—"

"You and your mother?"

The nurse burst in without knocking. This time she had the big attendant with her. "That's all the visiting for today. Franz, will you show Miss de Long's friend to the front entrance? Miss de Long must have her treatment now."

FOURTEEN

When Emily stopped at the desk of the Hotel Hollywood to ask
for her room key she customarily inquired for her mail as
well. The desk clerk customarily said no, nothing for a Miss
Daggett, and nothing for a Mrs. Weiss either.

Now, why should that cause her heart to sink every
time? What was she expecting? Did she really think Adam
would answer her letter? Dear Emily, I am consumed with
regret, I must have you back. Agnes Gelert is nothing to
me. Say you forgive me and I will crawl back to you on hands
and knees across the burning desert.

But no, never a letter from him. Time to face facts:
Adam was no longer the man she married, the man who
first won her heart by wrapping her in a sable coat. How
fleeting had been the comforts of that coat. In less than a

season he sold it again to finance Melpomene Pictures; now that, too, was gone.

Tonight as she came into the lobby, enduring the stares of the old lizards, Emily decided not to ask for her mail at the desk. It was clearly futile, as futile as asking herself again and again the question that had no answer: Why would Adam—why would anybody?—prefer Agnes Gelert to her?

Was Agnes sweeter and kinder? No, she was ill-tempered and cruel. Was Agnes more witty and clever than Emily? Again, no. Dull as a sack of potatoes. Did she have money? Not that Emily knew of. Was Agnes prettier? Not in the face; not really. Her chest was bigger. Maybe Adam liked that. Could it be that Agnes was better in bed? It seemed so unlikely. When he was with Emily Adam had always expressed the highest degree of enthusiasm.

Emily was forced to conclude that her husband had gone mad. How else to explain such a completely irrational choice? If that were the case, if Adam had lost his reason, it would be appropriate for Emily to fly to his side and support his recovery.

She imagined herself arriving in Ciudad Juárez, inquiring for her husband and Agnes Gelert, the movie star, the natives directing her to some stinking fly trap. Kicking the door open. Finding the two of them in their underwear cowering up against the headboard of their sordid bed.

Pulling Billie Burke's pearl-handled gun on them. Shooting Agnes in her big chest.

Blowing Adam's handsome chin away.

That was probably what happened to McHenry. Emily considered the scene in his bedroom, the manly wallpaper, the bloodstain, a huge splatter, little drops going off in all directions, the puddle on the floor. She imagined McHenry lying in the puddle with half his skull shot off. It could have been Adam.

For that was why people killed the ones they loved. Disappointment. Disappointment so deep that the other person seemed to lose all humanity and become monstrous, deserving of annihilation. Fit only to be squashed like a cockroach.

Wasn't Mrs. Swaine her sister after all, under the skin?

"Miss Daggett?" The desk clerk was waving an envelope at her.

"Yes?"

"I have a note for you. A man was here earlier and left it."

The handwriting on the envelope was uncomfortably familiar. Emily had the presence of mind to thank the desk clerk before she scuttled away to her room, out of sight of the clerk and the resident lizards, to open the envelope. It was from Adam. Here? Adam was here?

Emily,
I must speak to you. Be here at the hotel at eight o'clock this evening.

Adam

Adam was here. He knew where to find her. Well, of course he did. Hadn't she sent him a letter telling him? But this note. It was not affectionate. It was not apologetic. It could even be said to be bossy. Arrogant. *Be here.* She flew to the mirror, pinched her cheeks to dispel pallor, thought: Two hours. What would he say to her? What would she say to him?

Two hours of waiting like a fly in a spiderweb.

No. She would not be here at eight o'clock. On the contrary, she would very carefully contrive to be somewhere else.

She rearranged her hair, put on a nice fresh dress, and went down to the desk. "Tell me," she said. "Is there someplace where a respectable girl can go and have a little fun in the evening? I don't mean a saloon or a dance hall, but someplace—"

"Santa Monica Pier, honey."

Where Ross McHenry's body washed ashore. "But I don't fish."

"It ain't for fishing. It's an amusement park. Music. Rides. Hot dogs. Lemonade. Beer if you want it. Fresh sea air."

"How does one get there?"

"Streetcar."

"Sounds good." She peeled a greenback from her stash and handed it over. "If a gentleman comes looking for me, you don't know where I am."

"Mum's the word," said the desk clerk.

The gaudy stimulations of the Santa Monica Pier were just the thing for driving care away. High above the crashing waves of the Pacific (where Ross McHenry's corpse had evidently rolled undetected for weeks) a band concert was in progress, the musicians, spiffy in their red uniforms, playing the "Skater's Waltz." Couples were waltzing to it.

Children, sticky with cotton candy, ran and shouted. Gulls screamed and wheeled overhead.

Emily boarded the carousel and rode a huge, beautifully painted horse for two turns, up and down, up and down. The sea breeze pulled her hair loose from its pins under her hat. In this crowd of merry strangers she felt completely alone, and it was a pleasant sensation.

She never thought of trying to catch the brass ring, but somebody on the horse behind her snagged it; all the people cheered. She turned to see Chicago Eddie Green, laughing and waving the ring. Eddie Green had dimples! Who would have thought it? She almost didn't know him in his street clothes, well tailored, expensive, almost up to Adam's standards. Odd that a chauffeur should dress so well. But the diamond stud in his right earlobe gave him away; it was Eddie, for certain. Helping people feel good must be a lucrative way to supplement one's income.

Handsome as he was, Emily was not altogether pleased to see him. Something about Eddie Green was off-putting, she couldn't say what; it might have been the diamond, or the stuff he put on his hair, or the half smile he perpetually wore that was very close to a sneer. When Carl Laemmle wasn't in the studio Eddie Green looked at everybody there as if they had no clothes on, and not just the women. Still, Holbert Bruns said he knew things they should know, things she could pump him about. For one thing, Eddie Green still hadn't told her where he was on the night of the murder.

The carousel slowed and stopped. Here was Emily's chance to act like a real detective. Eddie Green handed her down off the carousel horse. "How'd you like a ring?" he said, holding it out.

"No, thank you."

"How about a dance, then?"

"I'd like that." He took her in his arms and they waltzed to the "Beautiful Blue Danube." Eddie was a good dancer, if you didn't mind the smell of hair oil.

"Where's your friend?" he said.

"Mr. Bruns? Working. What are you doing here?"

"I always come here on Saturdays. It's the best place in town to find a pretty girl."

"A different one every Saturday."

"You bet. Want a hot dog?"

"I'd love one."

"Mustard?"

"Please." As he retrieved some change with difficulty from his skintight pants Emily reflected that Eddie reminded her a little of Bruns. Not the fit of his clothes, certainly, but the air he had of being dangerous, that whiff of brimstone.

She glanced at the public clock. In fifteen minutes Adam would be showing up at the hotel, expecting her to be waiting for him, all obedience, as usual. But things were different now, as Adam would soon find. Emily was no longer his woman. Of course, he might have something important to say. Well, whatever it was, she would hear it at her own convenience.

The sun was sinking in the sea. "Let's take a walk," Eddie said.

"On the beach?"

"Good a place as any." Emily hesitated, but plenty of other people, couples and families with children, were strolling down there on the sand; it wasn't a dark alley, exactly.

Down off the pier the breeze dropped to almost nothing. Their feet sank in the soft sand. Emily thought of taking her shoes off, but decided it would be grossly improper, even for a woman of the theater. After all, she hardly knew this man. So they ambled along where the sand was still firm and wet from the falling tide, skipping sideways from time to time to keep the occasional wave from wetting their shoes. They hadn't gone very far before a swarm of little biting flies attacked them.

"Walk faster," Emily said. "Maybe we can outrun them."

So much for ambling. Eddie lengthened his stride; Emily could barely keep up with him.

"You're regular," Eddie said, for no particular reason that she could see. "Not like some of them dames in the studio."

"Thank you. You're kind of nice yourself."

"Don't believe the stories they tell about me."

"What stories?"

"Different ones. Lies, most of them. You may have heard things, but I ain't got nothing to do with any snowball ring."

"What's a snowball ring?" In the bushes on the bluff above the beach a dog began to bark.

Eddie stopped walking abruptly. "Let's get out of here. Dogs make me nervous."

"Wait!" Emily said. The last rays of the sun were falling on a flight of steps leading upwards from the beach.

Curiously decorated tiles were set into the risers. This was the house of the snapshots.

The barking grew louder, more savage.

"No, come on," Eddie said, pulling on her sleeve.

"But—"

"Who's down there?" It was the resonant voice of Alma Kazanow. A flashlight beam moved over the sand.

"Oh, Christ," Eddie muttered. Emily pulled her hat brim in front of her face as the flashlight beam swept toward them.

The dog growled; Alma Kazanow barked. "This is a private beach. Leave now, before I set my—you!"

"Take it easy, lady. I never saw you before in my life," Eddie said. Satan was on a lead, but he was straining at it, snarling and slavering. Eddie took Emily by the arm. "Come on, sweetheart. You heard what the lady said. It's a private beach."

They backed away from the steps into the darkness, then turned and ran, pounding along the damp sand in their dress shoes as though they cared nothing for them. When they could no longer breathe, when they could no longer hear the dog, they paused in their flight, gasping.

Emily emptied out her shoes. She was fairly certain that Mrs. Kazanow hadn't recognized her under the hat, one of her biggest. But as for Eddie—"Does that woman know you?"

"No. Why should she know me?"

"Why are we running?"

"I told you. Dogs make me nervous."

"You shouldn't run away from dogs. It only makes them more vicious."

"Thanks. I'll try to remember."

They walked on; the entrance to the amusement park came in sight. Suddenly Emily thought of Adam. He was waiting for her at the hotel, wracked with guilt, convulsed with repentance, prepared to fling himself at her feet and beg forgiveness, and she wasn't there for him. "I think I'm ready to go home now."

"Can I give you a ride?"

"No thank you, Eddie, I'll take the streetcar."

The same desk clerk was on duty when Emily rushed into the lobby. He looked up, saw her, and said, "Your friend didn't wait."

She turned away, getting lip rouge on her white glove. Suddenly she saw Holbert Bruns planted among the ferns and retired old lizards, with his face hidden behind the daily *Examiner*. She recognized his bony knees about the same time that he folded up the paper.

He was quite cross. "Where have you been?"

"I've been to the Santa Monica Pier, dancing with Chicago Eddie Green," she said, just to see what his reaction might be.

At first it was puzzlement. "Why?"

"You said I should try to discover what he knew about the murder."

"And did you?"

"No, but I found the beach house that was in those pictures of Ross McHenry." Several of the lizards looked up at the mention of McHenry's name. Emily lowered her voice. "It was about a quarter of a mile north of—"

"You went walking after sunset on a deserted beach with Chicago Eddie Green."

"The beach was hardly deserted, Mr. Bruns. There must have been—oh, I don't know—"

"Miss Daggett, I knew you were inexperienced when I hired you, I knew you were impulsive, but I had no idea you were mentally defective."

She stared at him. "Mr. Bruns. Was it not you who told me, 'If you're going to be a detective you must get as close as you can to the suspects and listen to all they have to say'?"

"I said that?"

"I would have thought that Eddie Green was as suspicious a character as anybody we're investigating. He deals in dope. He chases women. He chases men. Dogs chase him. I have come to believe that he's the man Boris said used to visit Ross McHenry on Friday nights. That would put him right on the scene at the time of the murder. If he invites me to take a closer look at him, what sort of detective am I if I refuse the opportunity?"

"A live detective. A detective with her personal reputation intact."

"Don't be silly."

"We'll continue this conversation tomorrow." He went away to his room in high dudgeon. The lizards gazed after him, hugely entertained. They took a great deal more delight in the scene than did Emily.

FIFTEEN

The next morning, when the good people of Los Angeles were in church and the others were sleeping off the exertions of Saturday night, Holbert Bruns called all his lady detectives to meet him at the IMP studio, which was empty of everyone but the watchman. He herded them into Carl Laemmle's conference room, a featureless chamber next to the Great Man's office, with cinder block walls, a linoleum floor, a conference table, and a number of mismatched chairs.

The conference table was someone's discarded dining table, marred with drinking glass rings and narrow black burn scars from long-ago abandoned cigarettes. Rumor had it that the conference table in Universal's new studio was to be made from Honduran mahogany. The chairs would all match, and there would be ashtrays. When at last the contracts were signed and the mergers completed, Universal would be the acme of luxury. It was said that Carl Laemmle was pursuing a cook for the new commissary who could make chicken soup just like his mother's. These joys were for another day.

They took their places around the table. Bruns sat at the head, of course; he was in charge. Emily sat at his right hand, her notebook and pencil at the ready. Etta and Wanda jostled for the place at his left hand until the superior force of Etta's bottom captured the seat. Gertrude sat at the foot of the table and directed her entire attention directly across at Holbert Bruns. Not for the first time, Emily noticed her lustrous eyes; not for the first time, she thought, This girl ought to be in pictures. It struck her that Gertrude was a natural for Trentoni. That poor creature in the sanitarium would never be well enough to do Trentoni's part.

While the actresses sorted out their places Holbert Bruns busied himself with lighting his pipe. He was scarcely speaking to Emily, still sore at her for strolling the beach with Chicago Eddie Green. Personal and professional autonomy, my aunt Fanny. Turning a cold shoulder to Emily, who only yesterday had been his most valuable assistant, he spoke directly to the Vine Street Irregulars:

"Now, ladies, I want you to tell me what you found out."

"We found out plenty," Wanda said. Gertrude continued to fasten him with her limpid gaze while the other two worked at looking competent and wise. Emily took notes.

Etta told her story first. "When we got to Krotona we split up, so as to cover more ground and not attract suspicion. I went to Ross McHenry's house. Did you know his yard boy is moving out? He got a job acting in the movies."

"Yes, I knew that," Bruns said. "He's one of my suspects."

"But what a man," Etta said. "What a marvelous physic. He's taking me to dinner again tonight."

"Good for you, honey," Wanda said.

"Yes, isn't it? I love a man with a job."

"Was that as far as you got?" Bruns asked her.

"I got far enough." Everyone stared. "Well, I can't sleep with Wanda the rest of my life."

Bruns cleared his throat. "I meant with investigating the situation at Krotona."

"*I* got pretty far," Wanda said. "You heard that the Women's Christian Temperance Union broke up Feeny's, right? They're still padlocked. So we had to go straight to Krotona after we left you. So I went all over casing the neighborhood. Say, it ain't as dry as you might think in the Hollywood Hills. Do you know there's a speakeasy right on Vine Street, about half a mile from the main hall of Krotona? I don't know why those people have to come all the way into town to close the saloons. So anyway I met the most interesting woman there. She works for the *Los Angeles Examiner*."

Bruns dropped his pipe. "Not—"

"It's okay, I didn't tell her a thing."

"I certainly hope not," Bruns said. "Did any of you try to talk to Alma Kazanow?"

"Yes. I did," Gertrude said.

"And did you have any success with her?"

"I haven't been on the stage all these years for nothing, Mr. Bruns." In a high, girlish voice, Gertrude mimicked herself, with gestures: "'Oh, Mrs. Kazanow, I feel so certain that you and the Krotonans have the answer to the deepest questions of my heart and spirit.'" Then in Alma Kazanow's rich alto: "'Why, certainly, my dear, come in and have a glass of mineral water.' We became great friends. She's a fascinating person, by the way. She read my fortune."

"Tarot cards?"

"Yes. She said I had a benefactor who walks with death. Who do you suppose she meant?" She looked from Bruns to Emily and back again. Emily wrote her words down, trying not to think about who it was that walked with death or why everyone she knew seemed to get along so well with her enemies. "Also we're going to the beach together this afternoon," Gertrude said. "And it's the servants' day off. A word to the wise: La Kazanow will be away from her house between one and five, in case you want to drop around and investigate."

"Well done, Miss Canty," Bruns said.

"Did you see anything of Mr. Kazanow?" Emily asked her.

"They aren't living together. She told me that. He's been staying at the Los Angeles Athletic Club ever since she realized that their marriage was a cosmic blunder."

While Emily's mind roamed off on the theme of marriage as a cosmic blunder, Bruns turned to Wanda. "Did you spend the whole afternoon drinking with Hester Mink in the roadhouse, or did you by some chance find out something about Ross McHenry's murder?"

Wanda scratched a match on her shoe and lit up a cigarette, a Lucky Strike, the same brand that Adam smoked. "He disappeared on April twenty-fourth, right?"

"That's right. Four weeks ago Friday."

"After I had a couple of snorts with the newspaper lady I went around and talked to the neighbors on the street behind Ross McHenry's house. I said I was doing a survey for the city. If you keep your face straight and hold a notebook in your hand people will believe anything you tell 'em." She picked a bit of tobacco off her tongue. "One of the neighbors—the bald-headed guy in the apron, right? He had a Model T in his driveway. I think his wife was out. Funny they didn't have a maid to wash the dishes, living in a neighborhood with movie stars."

"Yes. Funny," Bruns said. "Go on."

"Mr. Blanco, he said his name was."

"And?"

"He heard a lot of noise that night. He wasn't sure what it was. After that he saw a man and a dog."

"A man and a dog."

"Actually what he said was, 'I saw a man running pell-mell through my yard, pursued by a giant hound.'" Emily wrote: Eddie Green? Fear of dogs?

Bruns said, "How literary. The hound of the Baskervilles?"

"He didn't say. So I went to the next house. The man and the wife were both home. They hadn't heard or seen anything. Except maybe some shots. Or backfires. Or it might have been two cats fighting, knocking over the garbage."

"Was that all?"

"There was one other house. I knocked on the door and a man answered, kind of a tough-looking guy in his shirtsleeves. He said he heard a car backfiring that night. When he looked out he saw a dog and a shadowy figure running. He thought the figure was a woman."

Mrs. Kazanow? Emily wrote. Dog? Mrs. Swaine? But Mrs. Swaine used a cane and walked with a limp. How fast could she actually run?

"Or a man. Or a woman wearing pants. Someone running."

Bruns was silent for a long time, staring into the bowl of his pipe.

Emily said, "Babette de Long assured me that her mother killed him. That's her story. On the other hand, the girl is raving mad."

"Why would Babs's mother want to kill him?" Bruns said.

"They were married, I think. Babs claims to be their daughter."

"The British daughter?"

"They were Canadians, evidently. British subjects, hence the British passport. What she says could be true."

Murdering one's runaway husband made perfect sense to Emily, but Bruns couldn't see it. "You might just as well say it was Alma Kazanow. The dog could have been running with her rather than chasing her."

"If it was Alma Kazanow," Emily said, "maybe she has the missing gun. I was thinking that she might have come back to get it that day when she found me in the house with Boris."

"Not Mrs. Swaine?" Bruns said.

"Mrs. Swaine took only the picture of Babs. She didn't seem to be looking for anything else. Of course she might have had the gun already."

Bruns said, "Somebody should go back to Mrs. Kazanow's. Miss Rose! Would you like to go back up to Krotona this afternoon and search Mrs. Kazanow's house for Ross McHenry's gun, while Miss Canty keeps her busy at the beach? It's a Browning semiautomatic, like mine. Also see if you can find any personal letters to Mrs. Kazanow from Mr. McHenry."

"No."

"Why not?"

Wanda crossed her legs at the knee and stubbed out her cigarette. "I got a good look at that dog of hers. The hound of the Baskervilles was nothing to that one."

"Miss Daggett. Perhaps you can do it."

Their eyes locked in a cold blue stare. "The dog doesn't like me either, Mr. Bruns."

"I'll give you something for the dog. Uncle Holbert's special sleeping steak."

The drugged steak fitted neatly through the mail slot of Alma Kazanow's house, landing with a greasy plop on a pile of her mail. Alma would have cockroaches as a result of getting grease on her papers, Emily reflected, but what of it, she had servants, she had money, she could hire exterminators. The dog stopped its frenzied barking and began eating the steak. Emily could hear him munching and slobbering. Good.

While the drug was taking effect she went to canvass the neighbors, planning to return when Satan was unconscious. To assist her in her inquiries she took the group shot from McHenry's publicity folder. All the faces showed clearly.

A maid in uniform opened the door of the house next to McHenry's house. Emily produced the photograph. "Have you seen any of these people in the neighborhood in the last month or so?"

"Yes'm. That's Ross McHenry. He live next door."

"Any of the others? Look carefully."

The girl looked very carefully and shook her head.

And so it went. One by one the neighbors all identified Ross McHenry, but nobody recognized any of the others.

Until Emily came to Mr. Blanco. She found him in his yard polishing a fender of his Model T Ford. "Hi, there. I'm conducting a survey."

"Another one?" He stopped his polishing. His rag was khaki and had a black stripe of appliquéd braid up the middle.

"The city is keenly interested in the opinions of the residents of the Hollywood Hills." There were holes in Mr. Blanco's polishing rag, almost like tooth holes. And a brownish stain on it, too.

"What does the city want to know this time?"

"Where you got that rag."

He shrugged. "Found it in the yard last week."

"Is that a bloodstain?"

"Beats me. Are you sure you're from the city?"

She groped in her handbag. "I'll give you two bits for it."

"It's yours." The exchange was made.

"One other thing. Have you noticed any of these people in the neighborhood in the last month or so?" She held out the photograph. He took it and held it at arm's length, squinting.

"Yeah," he said finally.

"Who?"

"That's Ross McHenry. He lived right behind me."

"Any of the others?"

"Was there something fishy about McHenry's death?"

"No, we're simply making a survey of—"

"Because I read in Hester Mink's column just now that he was murdered by his drug pals."

"I don't know that he had any drug pals. Could you just look at this—"

"Snowball ring, she said. I don't guess a nice lady like you would even know what that is."

"You're right. I wouldn't. How about taking a look at this picture, seeing whether you can—"

"That guy." He put a dirty finger on the chauffeur in the doorway. "He's the one who was running away that night I heard the shot. Mrs. Kazanow set her dog on him."

"You heard a shot?"

"Yeah, didn't I mention that? Shot, backfire, something. Anyhow it went *bang*! And here comes this guy tearing through my petunia bed with that big dog after him. Was he the killer? Hey, wait a minute, did I just sell you a piece of his pants?"

"I don't know," Emily said. "You're sure this is the man you saw?"

Mr. Blanco smirked at her. "The moonlight was glinting off the diamond in his ear."

Emily could have gone back to Holbert Bruns right then and turned over all this useful evidence. The crime was solved. Mrs. Swaine shot Ross McHenry when she found him with Eddie, and while she and her daughter disposed of the body, Eddie ran away from the scene. This was the scenario that fit the facts. A visit to Alma Kazanow's house was all but pointless now.

Nevertheless, Emily had gone to the trouble of drugging Alma Kazanow's dog; to back out of breaking into her house would be to waste all that dope. Something was waiting in that house to be discovered. Alma Kazanow knew more than she was telling about the murder. Look how she tried to intimidate Emily. At the very least she was guilty of relaying vague threats against her through Gertrude, presuming she had any idea that Gertrude was an associate of Emily's. Besides, she was Howie's wife. Yes, she richly deserved to have her house broken into. At the end of this chain of reasoning Emily went back to Alma's front stoop, thankful for the cover of shrubbery.

The sound of snoring dog came clearly through the mail slot. Emily knocked on the door, just in case. No reply. More snoring. She wiggled her lock pick in the lock the way that Holbert Bruns had shown her.

For no reason that she could think of Emily had an uncanny feeling that Bruns was right, and Ross McHenry's Browning was somewhere in that house, although why that should be, when Mrs. Swaine was almost certainly the one who killed McHenry, Emily couldn't have said. Perhaps Alma Kazanow took the gun to blackmail Mrs. Swaine. She could see the gun in her mind's eye, sense that it was somewhere in the house. Something about Alma Kazanow's establishment encouraged clairvoyance: the heavy smell of jasmine, the soft, subdued light, the blood-colored draperies with their beaded trim. Who else but Alma Kazanow could have taken the gun? Who else had a key to Ross McHenry's house? Aside from Boris, that is, and Mrs. Swaine, and Little Babs. And all the other Krotona ladies. And maybe Chicago Eddie Green, who would not willingly come up here, at least not since the news of McHenry's death became public.

The dog lay stretched on the flagstone hearth, deep in slumber. Bruns really knew his stuff. Emily began her search by looking in the card table drawer, figuring that since that was where McHenry kept the gun in his house, Alma Kazanow might be inclined to do the same. Her hopes were dashed; nothing was there but cards and incense.

Then the telephone on the writing desk rang, once, twice. Silly to be so startled; no one was home. And yet somebody was home. Upstairs she heard coughing and the shuffling of feet.

Emily flew to the French window behind the sofa, pushing aside the draperies. The latch was stuck. She barely had time to conceal herself when someone came trotting briskly down the stairs. The phone rang a fourth time. Even through the thick velvet draperies Emily could smell bay rum.

"Hello?" Howie Kazanow wasn't supposed to live here anymore, and yet that was certainly his voice. "Oh, hello, you silly son of a bitch. What can I do for you this time?" Whatever the silly son of a bitch had to say caused Howie to break into uproarious laughter. "Not a chance, my boy. Alma's suing me for divorce. Her lawyers have got everything I own tied up in a knot." More chatter on the other end of the line. "I don't care how many camels are involved, sport, it's a nonstarter. There's no money here." Another pause. "Same to you, fella." He hung up.

A clinking of bottles and glassware, a sound of gulping, and then a rattling of the very drawer where Emily had been searching only moments before. A muttered curse. Whatever Howie was looking for in the drawer, it wasn't cards or incense.

And then the front door burst open.

"What are you doing here?" cried Alma. For a horrible moment Emily thought that Alma with her second sight had spotted her behind the window curtain. But, no, she was talking to Howie.

"I live here, my dear, in case you've forgotten."

"No, you don't. I threw you out."

"You know I can't stay away from you, Alma."

"You're drunk."

"Drunk on your charms, my sweet."

"Howard, try to control yourself. This is no longer your home. I thought my lawyers had made that clear."

"Damn your lawyers. This is still my home. You're still my wife, Alma. Darling, don't push me away. I can't go on without you."

"It's over, Howard. Don't embarrass yourself."

Emily was becoming embarrassed, and no one even knew she was witnessing all this. She bit her lip. Would the day ever come when Adam begged her to take him back? How would the scene go? Could she bring herself to be as cruel to him, the companion and friend who had shared her bed for years and years, as Alma was being to Howie?

Yes. It would be good to make Adam as unhappy as he had made her. Howie probably deserved this. Men deserved everything that happened to them. Footsteps clicked across the tile. The scratch of a match, the smell of jasmine incense. Alma didn't smoke; people who didn't smoke had to comfort themselves somehow in times of trouble. Why not with incense? Howie was weeping now, following Alma around the room like a dog. "Is it the money? I can give you money. I have plenty of money. It's all yours. I want you so."

"Howard. Listen to me. I have found a life that you can never share, on a plane that you can never achieve. The coarse stuff that our life was made of is in the distant past for me."

"I thought you liked it."

"I'm a different person now. I have different needs."

"No, you're not. You're still my Alma. Just once more, won't you let me—" Sounds of lurching, and then something heavy fell on the sofa. Two somethings, Howie and Alma. Howie's voice, muffled: "At last. I'm home at last."

"Aagh. Let go—" A struggle. Pop, rattle, and a long necklace's worth of beads splattered across the floor in all directions, some of them striking Emily's foot. Alma broke free and moved away from the sofa. "You clumsy brute! Get away from me before I call the servants."

"Go ahead and call them. I'll show them who's master in this house." Of course, the servants were out, Emily reflected, unless Gertrude was wrong about that, too. She felt for the door handle, twisted it cautiously. The door still refused to budge. There must be a lock.

"I'll call the police, then. I'll set the dog on you. Satan! Wake up! Bite him! What—oh, God, Howard! Satan is dead!" Dead? How much dope did Bruns put in that meat?

"I think he's still breathing, dear," Howie said. "But he's—"

"Poisoned! Someone has given my dog poison! That horrible little man with the diamond earring. First Ross and now this."

"Carl Laemmle's chauffeur? Why would he poison your dog, my darling? Here, it's all right. I can feel his breath."

"That man could be here! He could be hiding somewhere in this house!" Alma Kazanow began to shriek and babble incoherently. Was she begging her husband to call the police, or not to call the police? Unwilling to wait around and see, Emily fumbled frantically for the latch. There must be a latch.

SIXTEEN

Completely absorbed in the fate of the dog, the Kazanows didn't notice when Emily at last found the latch and escaped through the French window. She closed it softly behind herself and made a direct beeline for the Vine Street trolley. She didn't run; Bruns wouldn't want her to run; she strolled, making believe she had every right to be where she was, tra la la, and hoped that no one would challenge her. She was in luck. No one did.

Emily was not looking forward to explaining to Holbert Bruns exactly what had happened in Alma Kazanow's house. First of all she would have to tell him that she hadn't had time to find any personal papers, much less the Browning, that she hadn't even been able to look upstairs, because contrary to what Gertrude had told them Howie Kazanow was still there, or there again. Then she would probably have to mention the telephone call. It was Adam who called Howie. It had to be Adam, whining to that horrible person for money for camels.

Then she would have to show him Eddie's ripped pant leg and endure a lecture about what a bad character he was and how she must have been insane ever to go near him.

As it happened she was spared the necessity of giving an account of herself to Bruns, at least that evening, since Bruns wasn't in the hotel when she got home. She hung the pant's leg over the back of a chair in her room to dry and thought about the report she was to write.

Here was evidence placing Eddie on the scene. Was he the killer? Or was Little Babs right about her mother's guilt? Before Emily sat down at the typewriter to describe the afternoon's events she wanted to talk the case over with someone, if not Holbert Bruns then the girls, her fellow detectives. They could help her gain some perspective on what was happening before her observations solidified on the typewritten page.

She went downstairs and telephoned their boarding-house. Gertrude said to come on over; Wanda had a bottle of gin.

"He was here again," the desk clerk said as she hung up the hotel phone. "The man who wants to see you."

"Was he."

"Said he'd be back. Said for you to wait."

She gave him a quarter. "You haven't seen me."

"Where are you going?"

"For a walk." Why would she tell this person anything? He would tattle on her to Adam for six bits.

Emily did in fact go for a walk. The shingled Victorian boardinghouse where the girls were staying was half a mile from the Hotel Hollywood, a little way up in one of the canyons, a pleasant hike in her low-heeled shoes, after she took the stones out of them. Or, not stones. Purple beads, part of Mrs. Kazanow's broken necklace. They looked almost like real amethysts. She put them in her handbag.

Gin on an empty stomach was not an alluring prospect; Emily picked up some soda crackers and rat trap cheese at a grocery store along the way. The girls were happy to see her. Wanda, at least, was already well boiled by the time Emily arrived.

"So have you solved the case yet?" Wanda said.

"Not yet."

"Too bad," Wanda said. "I like your detective all right but I want to do a movie." She flopped down on the bed and closed her eyes. "Not getting any younger, you know."

Emily put the cheese and crackers on the dresser next to the matching comb, brush, buttonhook, and hair receiver, too flowery and cute to be anything but the property of the landlady. She glanced at her reflection in the mirror; the face that looked back at her seemed a bit thin and pale. She, too, was not getting any younger. Probably she should try harder to eat something from time to time.

"This is an engagement party, by the way," Etta said.

"Thanks to you, Boris and I can afford to get married. He's taken an apartment on Franklin Avenue."

"Good heavens. This is so sudden. I mean, congratulations. Have you set a date?"

"As soon as we can find a preacher."

"They've been calling all over town looking for a free chapel." Gertrude poured some gin in a small glass. "And a minister, or a justice of the peace, or something. Everybody's busy. You have no idea how many people want to get married in Los Angeles this week." She handed the stark drink of naked gin to Emily as if it were something nice. "Here you are. Down the hatch."

"Thank you. Best wishes to Boris and Etta." Emily held up the glass, saluted her friends, and took a swig. Gin wasn't really very good all by itself. She should have brought some fruit, or vermouth, or bitters. Something. When she got her breath back she gave them a progress report on the investigation. "I'm narrowing down the suspects, you'll be happy to know. Babs says her mother did it, right? But the neighbors saw Chicago Eddie Green running away after hearing a gunshot."

Wanda rolled over. "The running man was Eddie? Holy smoke."

"I'm pretty sure. Your man Blanco was using a piece of chauffeur uniform pants, all bloody and dog-mauled, for a cleaning rag. I think Satan chewed the leg off Eddie's pants on the fatal night."

"Why would Eddie Green want to shoot Ross McHenry?" Gertrude said.

"Don't know. He was selling him drugs, if that makes a

difference. They might have been lovers. McHenry liked men."

Gertrude shook her head. "McHenry, maybe, but Eddie?"

"Sure," Etta said. "Millie says Eddie chases everything. Women, men, sheep, watermelons—I know the type." She refilled her glass. "I grew up on a farm. What does Bruns have to say about it?"

"Can't find him," Emily said. "As for what he'd have to say, maybe he'd say—maybe he'd say Mrs. Swaine walked in on them while McHenry and Eddie were at it and shot her husband."

"The smart money is on Mrs. Swaine. Everyone hates her," Gertrude said.

"She and Ross McHenry were married?" Etta said.

"If we can believe the ravings of Babs."

"Tell me something, Emily. Who is this fellow Bruns, exactly?" Gertrude refreshed her drink. "Have you known him a long time?"

"Five years." Emily cut the cheese into pieces, clumsily, using the buttonhook. "When I met Holbert Bruns he was a Pinkerton operative. Working for the Pinkertons must have formed his character to a certain degree. He said to me not long ago that there was no law west of the Pecos. Where is the Pecos, anyway? I've always wondered."

"Someplace east of here," Etta said.

"Or maybe it's in Holbert Bruns's mind."

"His mind." Etta put a piece of cheese on a cracker.

"The Pinkertons have always considered themselves

beyond the law," Emily said. "A friend of mine explained it all to me years ago. On one side"—she gestured with the buttonhook—"you have the honest workingmen, and on the other side the bosses and the Pinkertons."

"Your friend sounds like a Red," Etta said.

"He is a Red. He went to Russia for the revolution. Boris knows him. Big Ed Strawfield."

"Whether he's a Red or not, he's right about the Pinkertons," Gertrude said. "I was just a tiny little girl in Homestead when the Pinkertons attacked the union men in 1892. They came up the Monongahela like an army, the murdering rats. My father lost his right hand."

Etta was aghast. "You mean a good friend of his, or his actual right hand?"

"His hand." Gertrude held up her own right hand and wiggled her fingers. "Bastards shot it off."

"Good heavens," Emily said.

"I think he's cute," Wanda said. Not asleep after all.

"We don't know that Holbert Bruns was with the Pinkertons at Homestead," Emily said.

"Maybe you should ask him," Gertrude said.

"He'd be too young," Etta said. "Wouldn't he?"

"Emily thinks he's cute, too," Wanda said. "Don't deny it, I saw how you looked at him. Pour me another one."

"Why don't you let me fix you some cheese and crackers?" Emily said.

"A Pinkerton," Gertrude said. "Just when I was beginning to like him."

"Don't hold it against him. We're in the twentieth

century now," Emily said. "It's been a long time since the Pinkertons were given to shooting honest laboring men in their beds."

Gertrude was not mollified. "All I know is, you can take a man out of the Pinkerton Agency, but you can't take the Pinkerton Agency out of the man."

"Will we have to shoot honest laboring men in their beds?" Wanda said.

"Only if it will help the studio," Emily said.

"I can't wait to start picking locks. Or fire a gun," Etta said. "Wish I had one. Emily is so lucky. Where did you get that pearl-handled thing of yours, Emily?"

"I took it away from a woman who wanted to shoot her husband's mistress," Emily said. Suddenly she remembered Adam, waiting for her at the hotel. Imagine that, she hadn't thought of him in ten minutes. How good it was.

Next morning at breakfast time Emily still had not found the words to frame her typewritten report to Holbert Bruns, and Bruns himself was still nowhere to be seen. She took the streetcar to the studio for the daily meeting with Carl Laemmle and found Bruns in Laemmle's office.

Laemmle, turning pink with optimism, rubbed his hands together at the sight of Emily. "Well. Have you seen our Little Babette? Can you tell me how soon she'll be ready to come back to work?"

"I don't know. She's a sick girl, Mr. Laemmle. No one can predict when she might recover. If ever. I'd really like to talk to her mother. She says her mother—"

"Ah, well, we can give her another week or so. Say, a fellow just left my office with a great idea for a movie, Miss Daggett. I'd like to know what you think of it."

"Oh?"

"It takes place in the desert, you see. We have this encampment with tents, and then some camels. Suddenly, the king of the Bedouins comes riding out of the sandy wastes, with a beautiful girl across the pommel of his saddle."

"Camels." There was something appallingly familiar about this scenario.

"Shouldn't be a problem, we can borrow them from Selig. Colonel Selig has a whole menagerie over on Eastlake Street, any animal you want. We could cast your friend Boris as the Bedouin king as soon as he gets finished with *Dark Star of India*—and we'll need a girl who looks good in harem pants."

"You're going to tell me you have someone in mind."

"The fellow who was just here has someone. Maybe you know him from the East Coast, his name is Adam Weiss. Used to own a studio in Fort Lee."

"I believe we may have met." Emily would not faint. Modern women did not faint. Still, she could feel the blood leaving her face.

Holbert Bruns cleared his throat in an effort to get the Great Man's attention, but Laemmle gabbled on, oblivious. "Mr. Weiss has a suggestion for an actress to play the part of Trentoni in *Jinks,* too, in case we can't get Babs to recover in time."

Emily's stomach dropped. "Not Agnes Gelert."

"Yes, how did you know? Agnes Gelert. His wife. You may remember her from *Lost Princess of the Islands, Divine Retribution,* and *Fair Maid of Jackson Hole.* I'm familiar with her work; she has a huge following. A nice screen presence, just the fresh young look we want. Here's a folder of her publicity portraits, if you want to—"

His wife? "I know what Agnes Gelert looks like. I'm afraid I don't think she would be a good choice for this picture, Mr. Laemmle." The Great Man kept a box of cigarettes on his desk. Emily took one and lit up, hoping for an effect of cool sophistication. Her eyes began to water, her head to swim. "Or any other picture. She has a terrible reputation. Evidently you've not heard."

"Does she really?"

"Yes. Drinks. Shows up late for work. Definitely on the skids. Not someone you want to hire at IMP." The cigarette tasted like burned garbage. She choked a little and put it out.

"I'm surprised to hear you say that," Mr. Laemmle said. "Mr. Weiss speaks very highly of her."

"Well, he would, wouldn't he? His . . . what did you say he called her? His wife."

"She ain't his wife?"

"Anything is possible, I suppose."

"So you don't like this dame. Do you like the desert picture?"

"Oh, I'm sure it's a great idea."

"But you don't want the wife for Trentoni."

"I wouldn't hire the wife, as you call her, to clean my toilet."

Emily was sorry for this outburst at once. It tarnished the aura of cool professionalism in which she had been trying to clothe herself ever since she came to Hollywood. When Laemmle glanced up and met Holbert Bruns's eyes a look passed between them that spoke volumes about masculine views on the frailty of women, the untrustworthiness of their judgments, the irrationality of their jealous passions. Bruns had the nerve to raise his shoulders a fraction of an inch, not quite a shrug but close enough to it to be insulting.

"Excuse me, gentlemen," Emily said. "I find that I must—" She rushed out, leaving them to think she had to take care of mysterious woman business. Some of the people in Laemmle's waiting room—tarted-up little actresses, badly dressed hustling men, and Millie, Laemmle's cheap receptionist—glanced at her as she passed through.

No one was in the hallway outside. It was a bad place to break down, a very public resonating chamber. Emily leaned against the wall under a lurid poster of King Baggot and Jane Fearnley in *Lady Audley's Secret* and gulped air, fighting for control of herself. Her breath slowed; she felt calmer. Probably she should see Adam, if only to find out what he was telling people. His wife. Why then was he was pursuing Emily so ardently? Had to be because he wanted something from her, maybe even something she was perfectly willing to give him, such as a pledge of her continued absence from his life. But she was so angry. So angry. She could scarcely control herself. What if she inadvertently pulled out Billie Burke's pearl-handled gun and drilled him?

A gloved hand touched her shoulder.

She turned to see Chicago Eddie Green in his uniform, smiling, showing the dimples. "You okay, sweetheart?"

"More or less."

He put his hand in his bosom and drew out a little bottle of pills. "Here, take one of these," he said.

"What is it?"

"Makes you feel good. Gives you the starch to carry on and do what you have to do."

But Emily already had the starch to do what she had to do, and it was to call Babette de Long's mother and ask to come and see her.

SEVENTEEN

Mrs. Swaine answered the telephone on the second ring, said she would be very pleased to talk to Emily, certainly, she should come right on out, and gave her directions to get to her house. Emily waited for the streetcar with the image before her of Adam—her own Adam, he used to be—abasing himself to beg for money from Howie Kazanow, or crawling from studio to studio to pander the dubious talents of that wretched little strumpet. She took her seat on the car and thought about being left penniless in Flagstaff with nothing but a telegram for an explanation.

Emily could sense the weight of the pearl-handled five-shooter in her handbag, feel its shape. Sisters. She and Mrs. Swaine were sisters. Their hearts were the same.

Babette de Long's mother welcomed Emily with a formal

afternoon tea: cucumber sandwiches, slices of cake, a bone china tea set in the Indian Tree pattern. She was not dressed in a lavender tea gown, which would have been Emily's choice if she had a beautifully decorated little house like Mrs. Swaine's where she could give people tea, but rather in the stark bombazine mourning dress of the funeral.

"Mrs. Swaine, I've come to talk to you about Ross McHenry. Your daughter told me everything."

"Poor Ross."

"How long were you married?"

"Ten years. We were never actually divorced; I suppose we're still married. Were still married. When he died." It was almost as if she still hadn't accepted his death, the way Emily still hadn't accepted, really, the fact that Adam had left her.

"That would make you his heir." A motive for murder?

"I don't want anything of his, except his daughter."

"Barbara."

"Yes. Babs."

"Tell me how you met."

"We grew up together in Kingston, Ontario. One summer when the Hagenbeck circus came to town we ran away together on a whim."

Emily remembered the circus in Eastport, her first sight of Ricky flying from trapeze to trapeze in a white leotard with spangles, his lean belly, his beautiful arms, his skillful hands. "A whim?"

"Not quite a whim. I was expecting Barbara. My father would have put me out of the house in any case. More tea?"

"Yes, please." The spoons were sterling silver from

Birk's. Not a wedding present, then. Pregnant runaways didn't get wedding presents.

"Hagenbeck's was a small traveling circus. Eventually we became the Flying Fazendas," she said. "And the Astonishing Angelonis as well, with a change of costume. We juggled flaming torches. Ross also worked as a clown, and I used to stand in front of a target for the knife-thrower. When the circus paraded into town I rode Mr. Hagenbeck's elephant. Barbara helped with some of the animal acts as soon as she was big enough, but she was still too young to be on the trapeze or the high wire. By that time we were working without a net."

"And then one day you fell." That was the reason for the walking stick.

"And then one day we both fell. My leg was never right again, and Ross hurt his back."

"He left you after that?"

"Not right away. Mr. Hagenbeck had to let us go; even with the drugs he took for the pain Ross wasn't good enough to carry the act by himself, and I was completely useless as a performer. Ross tried to find something to do in Toronto, but there was nothing. And then, as you say, he left me. Us."

"Because he couldn't support you?"

"That and because he realized—oh—" She looked for a long time into the depths of her teacup, thinking how to put it. "He realized it wouldn't do anymore for the two of us to be married."

"I see." The thing with the men. "What did you do after that?"

"Barbara had a gift for the stage. Her work was able to support both of us."

And to pay for silver spoons from Birk's. "So you never remarried?"

"I was very much in love with Ross, Miss Daggett. There was never any other man for me. But we married too young, before he knew, really, who he was. It was a mistake for me to come to Hollywood after him, I realized it almost at once. I'm sorry I ever did. Barbara became so attached to him, and he was such a—so irresponsible with her."

"What did he do?"

"He gave her drugs. I don't know why."

"Who was Mr. Swaine?"

"Swaine is my maiden name." She stirred her tea, grinding the spoon on the granules of sugar, and then looked up. "And Mr. Daggett?"

Emily smiled. "My father."

"What was your husband's name, my dear?"

"Adam Weiss." Emily hadn't spoken her husband's name since she left Flagstaff. Doing it now made her light-headed. She could feel her lips tingling unpleasantly.

Mrs. Swaine took Emily's hand in a warm, firm grip. "You'll recover. You'll see, your life will be better. Still I think you can understand why I wanted to change my name."

Emily finished the last sip of her tea. Stop making friends with this woman, she told herself. Interrogate her. Detect things. Take charge of this interview. "I understand a great deal about you, Mrs. Swaine, because our situations are similar, as you have observed. Sometimes I think that if I had it in my power to murder Adam Weiss I would do it without a second thought." Emily felt that this was true. It wasn't something she would have told most people.

Mrs. Swaine recoiled slightly. "Surely not."

"Your daughter told me everything, Mrs. Swaine, how you shot your husband, how she helped you dispose of the body."

"Shot him?" Mrs. Swaine passed her hand in front of her eyes, as though to brush away stray hairs or brush away confusion. "He was shot? I thought he was killed in a diving accident."

"He was shot to death in his bedroom on the night of April twenty-fourth. By you, your daughter says."

Mrs. Swaine put down her teacup and stared at Emily for a long time. Her face grew deathly pale. "My God," she said at last, and then, "Barbara is very sick, you know. Don't put a lot of stock in anything she says."

"There's corroborating evidence."

"Evidence? I wondered about that absurd rush to cremate his body—"

"Other evidence. Bloodstains in his room. Neighbors who saw someone running away."

"The twenty-fourth of April."

"Yes. It was a Friday."

"Oh." Mrs. Swaine looked at the tea cakes as though they had all become scorpions and spiders. "Oh. That explains—"

"What?"

"Nothing. And what are the police doing?"

"The police don't know. Mr. Laemmle wants it hushed up."

"I see. And he always gets what he wants, doesn't he? What are you going to do?"

"Find out the truth. As Mr. Bruns says, we have to know what actually happened before we can keep it quiet."

"Oh. Well, then. As you have me dead to rights, I might as well confess. Yes, I shot Ross. I went to see him that day and found him in bed with someone else."

"Who?"

"I don't know. Does it matter? I was, of course, out-raged, you can understand that, Miss Daggett, and so I . . . I shot him."

"And then you drove him to the ocean and threw him off a cliff? And Barbara helped you carry him?"

"If she says so, yes, that's how it happened."

"How did you get him to the ocean?"

"In . . . in a car, as you say."

"You have a car?"

"I borrowed it from the studio."

"You said to Eddie Green, 'I need to take a car so I can go and murder my husband.' Or did he help you? Was he bitten by the neighbor's dog while he was running away?"

"Eddie? Good heavens, no. I—I drove the car myself."

"That seems unlikely to me. Do you even know how to drive?"

"There's no need to be rude, Miss Daggett, I told you what happened."

"Where did you get the gun?"

"It was Ross's. He kept it in a drawer in the living room with his playing cards."

"What did you do with it afterwards?"

"I threw it in the sea."

And it subsequently reappeared in the card drawer. Sure it did. "Mrs. Swaine, I don't believe you."

She drew a long breath and stared at her folded hands. "You don't believe me because people don't really do things like that to each other, not to the people they love, Miss Daggett. You don't really want to murder your husband, do you? Not really."

Actually, yes, she did. But now she felt shame at having confessed it to this innocent woman.

EIGHTEEN

Emily found it difficult, typing up her report of the Swaine interview for Holbert Bruns, to phrase it so that his understanding of the event would be the same as hers, that Mrs. Swaine was guiltless, that she knew nothing about a murder until she heard of it from Emily, that Mrs. Swaine confessed to killing her husband in order to shield her daughter. She ended her report with bald, unsubstantiated statements: Mrs. Swaine is innocent, et cetera. Bruns would not trust her womanly intuition. He would chide her for jumping to unprofessional conclusions.

Eddie and the pants made for a more straightforward story. She mentioned the drugs, the rumors of bisexuality, and the chewed-up pant's leg, which artifact she enclosed with the report in a manila envelope addressed to Bruns.

Rumors and chunks of pants were okay in a detective's report; intuitions were not.

The sun was still high in the sky when Emily dropped the envelope at the hotel desk, an excellent time for a walk as long as one had the proper hat. She gave her key to the clerk. "I'll be out for a while," she said. "If that man comes back you haven't seen me." He looked expectant; she gave him another two bits.

Birdsong, butterflies, the scent of orange groves, the warmth of the afternoon sun, and an energizing walk to the boardinghouse where her friends lived. What could be nicer? As she climbed the hill the city of Los Angeles spread out behind her like a carpet she could turn and step on, or a juicy peach she could stretch out her hand and take. Big future here in detecting. She let herself play with the idea. What had Bruns been talking about? Did he want a partner, or someone to work his typewriter? Or something else entirely? But Emily didn't want another man, not now, not until her tangled feelings about the last one had been sorted out. Nor did she want a job outside of moving pictures.

Etta was sitting on the porch swing when Emily arrived, wearing a ribbon in her hair and a white eyelet frock, with her feet tucked up under her, gliding slowly back and forth. Wanda and Gertrude posed on either side of her in stylishly languid attitudes. What a pretty picture they made. Emily stretched her palms out toward them, thumbs together, and framed them with her hands.

"Lovely," she said. Too bad she hadn't a movie camera.

"Yes," Gertrude said. "We're lovely. We have to be. Etta is getting married in an hour."

"What?!"

"It's true," Etta said. "Boris got a license this afternoon."

"Where is the ceremony to be?"

"We looked all over town. We couldn't find anyplace at all," Etta said.

"So Eddie Green told me about all those flowers that Mr. Laemmle had delivered to the chapel in Hollywood Cemetery," Wanda said. "Tons and tons of lilies and white carnations. He said they were probably still fresh, so we thought, what a shame for them to go to waste."

"When did you see Eddie?"

"Oh, we . . . ah . . . he's a lot of fun, you know?"

Hollywood Cemetery? "Etta! You're not getting married in a funeral chapel?"

"Boris doesn't mind. He said, 'Why not? Marriage is a little bit like death anyhow.' What do you think he meant by that?"

"Boris is deep," Wanda said.

"We have to put an announcement in the paper," Etta said.

Gertrude cleared her throat and struck an attitude. "Miss Etta Mary Sweet and Mr. Boris Ivanovich Levin were united in marriage today at the chapel of Eternal Rest at the Hollywood Cemetery, the Reverend Mr. Dwight Wright of the Unitarian Church officiating. The bride was gowned in a lavish creation of embroidered white eyelet, and was attended by Miss Wanda Rose, wearing a frock of melon pink peau-de-soie sprigged with bottle green butterflies, formerly the property of the lovely Miss Emily Daggett. Miss Rose requested those present not to call her Baby Wanda. The lavish flowers were a gift of Uncle Carl Laemmle, laboring under the impression that everyone present was dead."

Marriage is death, Emily thought. Interesting notion. Boris might have something there. "Where did you find a Unitarian minister?"

"Living next door to Boris on Franklin Avenue," Etta said. "He's the nicest man."

"And who is to be best man?"

"Nobody," Gertrude said.

"Nobody?"

"You will remember that Alice Roosevelt had ten attendants at her wedding, and every one of them a handsome young man," Gertrude said. "No bridesmaids. Why can't we stand up for Boris? You're coming, too, of course, Emily. You and I will be his best man."

"Hasn't he any friends?"

"They're all on the East Coast," Etta said.

"Maybe Eddie will stand up with him," Wanda said.

Why not? Marry in a funeral chapel, attended by a killer. What better way to start off a life together?

In the event, it was Chicago Eddie who served as best man, looking altogether presentable in his Saturday night suit, celluloid collar, and striped silk tie, but still somehow uneasy. Maybe he was skittish at the idea of marriage. Maybe it was the overpowering smell of lilies and carnations. Maybe he was uncomfortable with the near presence of a minister of God, even a Unitarian minister. Or maybe he feared that if he came to God's attention at all he would be struck dead for the murderer he was.

As the sweet old words flowed from the minister's mouth Emily found herself thinking back to her own wedding in the Philadelphia City Hall. Myrtle Stirrup served as her bridesmaid, her good friend from the chorus of *Monkey Days*. Adam was saddened and perhaps offended that the press of Howie Kazanow's business engagements prevented him from coming and acting as his best man. Myrtle Stirrup's boyfriend did the honors instead. Emily could no longer remember his name. As for Myrtle, they lost track of each other years ago.

Emily and Adam's wedding party, like Etta's, was very small. No one from the family in Eastport came, not Emily's mother, who objected to the marriage, nor her brother, who was away at sea, nor any of her uncles, aunts, and cousins. Her mother had never really forgiven her for running off with Ricky. For Emily to marry Adam, a Jew, was the last straw for poor old Mrs. Daggett.

Adam's people didn't come to the wedding either. He never told her why, whether it was because she was a chorus girl, or because she was a Gentile, or because of some quarrel they had with Adam himself. No family came. They married with a surprisingly delicious feeling of being together beyond the pale. It was snowing. Emily wore the sable coat.

And they promised, as Etta and Boris were now promising, to forsake all others.

I hope I'm not going to cry, Emily thought. Crying at weddings is so trite. She was groping for a handkerchief when everyone suddenly began hugging and shaking hands. Boris and Etta were man and wife now. Wanda was helping herself to Carl Laemmle's carnations, grabbing handfuls from the white-painted baskets.

"Let's go, folks," Chicago Eddie Green said, taking the couple each by an elbow. "Train leaves in half an hour."

"You're leaving?" Emily was surprised. The wedding seemed unfinished. No reception? No cake? No ham, no caviar, no champagne?

"We'll be back next Monday when begins the filming," Boris said. "Not to fear." He kissed all the women and followed Eddie to the limousine.

"They're leaving?" Wanda said. "What about the wedding supper?"

"I guess they'll have it on the train," Gertrude said.

"I mean *our* wedding supper."

"We'll have to arrange it for ourselves," Emily said. "Feeny's serves food, don't they?"

"Feeny's hasn't reopened since the WCTU shut them down," Wanda said.

"How about that roadhouse on Vine Street, the one near Krotona?" Gertrude said.

"The one where Hester Mink likes to go?" Emily said.

"Right. The Red House."

"I don't know about food. They have pickled eggs and pig's knuckles," Wanda said. "And maybe the odd pretzel."

"That's good enough for me," Gertrude said. "Come on. The streetcar will take us straight there."

"Hope we don't meet Hester," Emily said.

NINETEEN

The Red House had a bar, a dance floor, a piano, and a cigar-smoking piano player with arm garters. It did not have a ladies' entrance. Hester Mink was nowhere to be seen. There were, as far as Emily could tell, no ladies present, and no gentlemen either. Five or six hard drinkers hunched over the bar in buffalo plaid shirts that came just short of their Levis, displaying the clefts of their bottoms all in a row. In the corner a poker game was going on. The scene looked for all the world like something out of one of Melpomene's Westerns, except for the clefts, which wouldn't have passed the censors. Eyebrows went up when the Irregulars came in, mostly the tweezed eyebrows of the girls at the end of the bar (clearly not ladies), but also the furry eyebrows of the barman.

"Here's a table," Wanda said. They occupied it. The barman came over, scowling. Emily thought he meant to throw them out until Wanda put money on the table. "Bring us a pitcher of beer, my good man."

"Oh, it's you, Miss Rose," the barman said. "You going to sing for us again?"

"After I have a drink, Jimmie," Wanda said.

"Your friends sing?"

"They dance," Wanda said.

"Swell!" A sort of smile appeared on Jimmie's battered face. He brought them glasses and a pitcher; they emptied the pitcher, he brought them another.

They got up and sang "Tell Me Pretty Maiden," "Shine On, Harvest Moon," "Smiles," and "Captain Jinks of the Horse Marines." After another round of drinks they danced the scandalous turkey trot while the piano player banged out a rag. Then they waltzed with the more attractive of the locals, and fended off the attentions of the rest. About suppertime, when things were getting really mellow, Emily thought it was time for her to leave, and she would have done it, too, the next time the door came around, if the floor hadn't risen up and hit her in the face first. Brown linoleum. An interesting pattern of squiggles.

The Irregulars picked her up and put her in a chair. She began to weep.

Gertrude was horrified. "Emily, what's wrong?"

"I'm going to kill Adam Weiss, the great love of my life. He betrayed me with a worthless trollop and I have to shoot him to death the next time I see him. It's so sad."

"I believe she's having a crying jag," Gertrude said. "Emily, have you eaten anything today?"

"Did I ever tell you how handsome he was? When he was rich he gave me a sable coat."

Gertrude said, "Supper, that's what we need. I almost forgot. Alma Kazanow is having a séance about now."

Wanda said, "Is she serving food?"

"How can she have a séance?" Emily said.

"She just is, and food as well, and I have an invitation. We're great friends, you know."

"*Chacun à son gout,*" Emily said.

"What?" Wanda said.

"*Fledermaus,* right?" Gertrude said. "I have a little culture, too. Would you like to come?" She brandished an engraved invitation at them.

"Sure, we wanna come," Wanda said. "Where is it? And what about supper?"

"She said there would be supper. It's at her house. About four blocks that way, I think." Gertrude waved in the direction of the door, narrowly missing Jimmie the barman as he passed with a tray of glasses.

The plan did not recommend itself to Emily. She said so, very slowly and clearly. "Gertrude, I believe we're all . . . stinko. Those people in the Krotona community don't approve of strong drink."

"Piss on 'em," Wanda said. "I wanna see a ghost."

And so off they went to the séance. The dry, cool air cleared their heads to a certain extent, to the point where Wanda stopped saying bad words and Emily was able to stand up straight. The event was already under way as they approached. Alma Kazanow, in full gypsy regalia, glided out of her front door.

"Where's she going?" Emily said.

"The actual séance is at Ross McHenry's house," Gertrude said. "They're going to try to contact the poor man's astral body."

Alma Kazanow crossed the street to Ross McHenry's front door, surrounded by twittering women, and let herself in. The Irregulars caught up with a handful of stragglers.

"Are you here for the séance?" one of the stragglers said.

"Why, yes," Gertrude said. "Marvelous, isn't it?"

"Yes, wonderful. And to think Mrs. Kazanow almost wouldn't do it. We had to bully her unmercifully, didn't we, Gladys?"

Gladys snickered. "Threatened to pull her membership. But who better to raise the astral body of Ross McHenry?"

"Who indeed?" Gertrude said.

"Dear Ross. You know, it was Alma who brought him into the community. We have so much to thank her for." The stragglers directed worshipful gazes in the general direction of McHenry's front door.

Emily thought of the scene in the bedroom. What about the smell? The bloodstains? "Why is it, again, that we're having the séance in Ross McHenry's house?"

They all began to babble. "He lived there. He lived there, my dear—"

"Everywhere you look, little things he saw every day—"

"Things he touched—"

"Still holding traces of his energy—"

"And, of course, dear Mrs. Kazanow is the only one among us who has any experience or skill in mediumship—"

"Theosophists don't normally do séances," Gertrude said. Clever girl, she must have been studying Mrs. Kazanow's books.

The women babbled on. "An oversight, I think. They add so much to the spiritual tone—"

"Before she joined our group, Mrs. Kazanow raised many spirits—"

"And of course she has the key to his house—"

"She's a house agent, you know—"

"Do let's hurry—"

"Wait. Did we miss the dinner?" Wanda said.

"There's some food left in Mrs. Kazanow's dining room. Watch out for the dog," the last straggler said, as she rushed into McHenry's house. So the Krotona ladies threatened to pull her membership. Could it be that Alma Kazanow was not in control of this event?

Wanda poked Gertrude in the ribs. "What did the soul say to the spirit?"

"I dunno. What?"

"Ah, Spirit," Wanda said. "And what did the spirit say to the soul?"

"Ah, Soul. Oh. I get it. Ha-ha."

"Ha-ha. I made you say asshole. 'Scuse me, I'm going to go find something to eat."

While Wanda drifted away into Alma Kazanow's unlocked house in search of food, Emily followed the stragglers into the house of Ross McHenry. Indeed Mrs. Kazanow was having to struggle mightily to dominate this gaggle of women.

"No, no, no, no, don't go upstairs. That will break the Kamic link. We must gather around the dining-room table and hold Brother Ross in our minds, all together." The table was round, a massive piece of mission oak. There were almost enough benches and chairs for everyone. Gertrude pushed in among the Krotona ladies, taking up little space because of her slim bottom and the modest brim of her hat. Emily elected to stand in the shadowy corner, out of Alma Kazanow's line of sight.

While Mrs. Kazanow placed eight candles in the middle of the table, someone pressed the light switch and the room became totally dark. "A candle for each planet," Mrs. Kazanow murmured. She lit them, casting a flickering glow on the faces of the circle of women. "Spirits are attracted to light and heat. Now we all take hands and close our eyes."

For a long time no one spoke. Emily became aware of a presence at her side. Her hand drifted into her bag, feeling for the reassuring shape of the pearl-handled revolver, but it was only Wanda standing next to her in the dark. She was chewing something. Smelled like chicken. But no, it wouldn't be chicken; these people didn't eat meat.

"Brother Ross," Alma Kazanow said. "Are you with us? Knock once for yes, twice for no."

Wanda knocked twice.

"I sense a malign presence. Begone."

Knock, knock.

Emily dug her elbow into Wanda's corseted ribs. Wanda dug back.

"We seek the astral body of Ross McHenry. Brother Ross, if you are with us, signify."

Knock. Muffled. Not Wanda this time.

"Brother Ross. I bring you the benison of your friends, the women of Krotona. We wish you rest in the afterworld."

Knock, knock.

Emily's hand closed around the beads lying at the bottom of her purse.

"Your spirit must move on to the next plane, Brother Ross. Let your being merge with the atma."

Knock, knock.

"Is your soul troubled?"

Knock.

"Ladies, let us all send a spirit of peace to Brother Ross that he may achieve the radiant glories of the heavenly world. Breathe in . . . breathe out . . ."

None of this seemed to Emily to be to the point. If it were Brother Ross knocking, clearly it was because he had something to communicate about the cause of his unrest, possibly even the name of his murderer.

"Send us a sign, Brother Ross, that you accept our blessings . . ."

No sign came; this was a cheat; Brother Ross would never accept such hypocritical blessings. Disgusted, Emily threw her handful of amethyst beads at the table. How they clattered.

"Lights!" Alma Kazanow screamed. The lights came

on. Mrs. Kazanow picked up the beads, looked at them, her face twisted with rage, turned and saw Emily standing behind her. Wanda must have gone for more of the chickenlike substance.

"You threw those beads. Where did you get them?"

"I don't know. I found them."

"You found them in Carl Laemmle's limousine, didn't you?"

"I really couldn't say."

"I knew it. That man."

"What man?"

"Cover up for him all you like, I know who my enemies are. And my friends, as well. Come, ladies." She rose and swept out of the house, her followers swirling after her, Gertrude among them. Key in hand, Alma Kazanow waited by the door. When Emily didn't move fast enough to suit her she shouted, "Come out!" Emily came out.

Mrs. Kazanow locked the door behind her. "In two minutes I will release the dog. Don't be here."

TWENTY

Good to know that she hadn't killed the dog, Emily reflected, leaping for the streetcar. Maybe the creature would return the favor some day. As she rode along in the nearly deserted car, sobriety began to creep over her, starting with her toes and fingers and proceeding upward to her throbbing head. By the time the car reached Hollywood Boulevard she had gathered enough of her wits to change to the line that would take her home to the Hotel Hollywood.

If she found Holbert Bruns waiting for her in the hotel she could explain to him face-to-face about Mrs. Swaine, about Chicago Eddie, maybe even about Mrs. Kazanow, to the extent that she knew anything about that strange woman. She could even take her courage in her hands and talk to Bruns about Adam, about her fear of murdering him the next time she saw him, maybe even ask his advice on whether under the circumstances she should actually be carrying a loaded gun around with her.

But he wasn't there. In a way that was good; Emily was spared the immediate necessity of trying to sober up and behave like a professional detective. Instead she could take deep breaths, think of herself on a rock by the ocean in Eastport, Maine, soaking up the rays of an August sun, twelve years old again and free of all worldly cares. Five or ten minutes of this exercise should certainly—

"Miss Daggett?" The clerk waved her over to the desk.

"Yes?"

"There's a telephone message for you from Mr. Bruns."

"What was the message?"

"He left word for you to go and meet him in Bryce Canyon, at the Union Rock Company quarry."

"Where's that?"

"It's in Griffith Park. There's a cave. Everybody knows where it is."

"I don't."

"His message says that Mr. Eddie Green will pick you up and drive you there. He knows how to find it."

"Mr. Bruns said that? Eddie would drive me?"

"That's what it says here. It says he wants you up there right away."

"Who took the message?"

"I don't know, miss. It was here when I came on duty."

The clerk seemed to expect a tip, so she tipped him, even though it didn't feel right, Bruns telling her to go off god-knows-where all alone with Chicago Eddie Green.

Emily couldn't think of any reason not to, other than that Eddie probably murdered Ross McHenry. (So he murdered Ross McHenry. Did that mean he necessarily had anything against Emily? Certainly not. He had never treated her with anything other than respect and friendliness.) And yet it seemed so unlikely that Holbert Bruns would tell her to drive to some remote cave with him. Bruns must have discovered something new about Eddie's trustworthiness. That he was an Eagle Scout, perhaps. Or maybe Bruns was setting some sort of trap for Eddie. In that case it was up to Emily to do her part.

"Call me when Mr. Green arrives," she said, and went up to her room to take a bromide and change her hat.

After the bellboy announced the arrival of Eddie Green, Emily found him waiting for her under the streetlight outside, polishing the windshield of the Cadillac with that same rag, the one that looked like an old torn pant's leg, the mate to the one with the tooth holes and bloodstains. Ripped from the same pair of pants, surely. Emily wondered whether she could decorously get a look at Eddie's leg, to check for dog bites. Probably not.

Seen fleeing from the murder scene, pursued by a dog. Clearly Eddie was the killer. Equally clearly, Bruns had something in mind for Eddie that was to take place at this quarry. Whatever it might be, he expected Emily to get him there.

"Hi, Eddie." She jumped in the front seat.

"Hiya, sweetheart. Where to?"

"Mr. Bruns wants me to meet him at the Union Rock

Company quarry in Bryce Canyon. He says you know the way."

"The cave?"

"I guess. Of course, if you're afraid to go up there this late—"

"Eddie Green ain't afraid of nothing."

"Nothing except dogs."

"Oh, yeah. Dogs." He pushed the ignition switch and the engine turned over.

"I'm afraid of heights myself. Is it very far up in the hills, this quarry?"

"Not too far. It's kind of out of the way, is all. No kidding, are you afraid of heights? I saw you in *Massacre at Bitter Wash,* the way you hung off that cliff. You wasn't acting?"

"I'm not really much of an actress. What I want to do is direct."

He laughed. "Good luck to you, sweetheart." It was a nice evening for a drive, soft and warm. As they passed through a shadowy orange grove Eddie pretended to mistake Emily's knee for the gearshift. She removed his hand, and he switched from being a fresh guy to being the tour guide.

"Now we're in Griffith Park," he said, steering the car onto a road that passed into a wood.

"Really."

"Yeah. There's a curse on it, you know."

"Go on with you."

"No kidding. Fifty or sixty years ago all this belonged to an old Spanish don with a little blind niece. Rancho Los Feliz, it was called. Happy ranch."

"And the don offended some witch, I suppose, so that she cursed it."

"No, the niece cursed it. The old don died, but while he was on his deathbed his neighbor came over and got him to leave it to him in his will. The niece got nothing, so she cursed the ranch and everybody who would ever own it. Three or four people died. Some of them went crazy."

"Good heavens. Who owns it now?"

"City of Los Angeles."

"I see."

"Explains a lot, right? Griffith gave it to the city after he found out it was cursed. But by then it was too late."

"So he's dead."

"No, he's still around. He got out of jail a couple of years ago."

"What was he in for?"

"Shot his wife."

"Poor wife."

"That's what the people in the city said. The old lady lived through it, but she lost an eye and her face is all scarred up. None of the swells will speak to Griffith anymore."

"They didn't give the park back to him, though, did they?"

"No, they didn't. Even so, they won't let him build a Griffith Observatory in the middle of it and put up a statue of himself."

"Why not? They didn't mind calling the park after him."

"What they said in the paper was, quote, 'We're not lost to all sense of decency.'"

"Refreshing in a city government. Eddie, take your hand off my knee."

"Sorry, sweetheart, I thought it was the gearshift."

"So. Do you believe in the curse of Griffith Park?"

"I believe people make their own luck. I know I make mine."

A road deeply rutted by gravel trucks led into the woods, and there before them was the quarry. Eddie pulled the limousine off the road, turned off the engine and the lights, and set the brake. In the dark the silence was absolute. Not even a cricket peeped.

If Holbert Bruns was there to meet her he was certainly very well hidden. It was true that there were plenty of places to hide. Heaps of crushed rock and digging machinery made hulking shapes in the murk. Beyond them was a deeper darkness. Was that the cave?

"Mr. Bruns?" she called. Nobody answered.

Emily could hear Eddie breathing next to her, and rather heavily. She began to regret sitting in the front seat. Aesthetic distance, that was what was required between her and Chicago Eddie Green, not warm closeness in the front seat of an automobile. The sound of his breath was—

"Hey, sweetheart, it's cold with the engine off. Why don't you let Eddie keep you warm till your friend gets here?" He slipped his arm around her shoulders.

She shrank away from him. "Uh, no thanks, Eddie, I think I'll—"

"Loosen up. You're in California now." He nuzzled her neck. "C'mon, sugar. You know you want it. Why else did you make me drive you up here?"

"I didn't!" She wriggled out of his grip and jumped over the car door into the pitch dark, tearing the hem of her skirt. "I didn't make you drive me up here! It was Holbert Bruns!" Rocks and stones got under her feet where she couldn't see them. She stepped carefully away from the car.

Eddie Green jeered at her out of the darkness. "So where's your boyfriend now, sweetheart? I think *you* got me to drive you up here, and then you got cold feet." He started laughing; let him laugh, as long as he didn't chase her into the bushes. He was still laughing when she found the entrance to the cave and ducked inside to wait for Bruns, who must have had something in mind, luring the two of them up there like that. The sound of Chicago Eddie Green's laughter echoed unpleasantly inside the hollow space.

Under no circumstances was Emily going to get back in that car with that man, not even to get back down the mountain. She'd rather walk. She began to feel around in her handbag for Billie Burke's pearl-handled five-shooter. If Eddie got out of the car and attempted to force his attentions on her she was prepared to shoot him in the knee. She was after all an excellent markswoman, capable of putting a hole in a tomato can at thirty paces. Or forty feet. Anyway, far enough.

As she was remembering what that felt like—how she took careful aim along the barrel, squeezed, squeezed the trigger, absorbed the recoil, admired the hole in the tomato can—an actual shot rang out.

The laughing stopped abruptly. A long silence, then

footsteps crunched on gravel and swished in the leaves. No light was visible, but someone was coming toward the cave.

Was it Eddie? Could it be Holbert Bruns? Emily thought of calling out, but if it was Eddie she would have more trouble on her hands, and if it was someone other than Eddie or Bruns. . . . She cocked the pistol; with a soft click the trigger dropped down.

She shrank back against the wall of the cave, trying not to think about spiders, aiming Billie Burke's pistol at the faint almost-light that was the mouth of the cave. Something dark moved into the cave's entrance. Whether to call out, shoot first, or cower and be still—as Emily attempted to choose among her options the shadow moved away again, crunching softly back toward the limousine. The sound of the engine starting up, the flash of the headlights; the Cadillac was driving away.

Emily waited a long time before moving. It felt like hours. At last she groped her way to the cave entrance.

"Mr. Bruns!" she called. No answer. "Eddie?" Nothing. By now the moon was out, and by its light she was able to discern where the road went. She started walking down the hill, keeping well away from the black depths that yawned from time to time first on one side of the road and then the other. Sometimes the road itself was absolute inky darkness, strewn with treacherous lumps of rock, or horse dung, maybe even bear dung. Griffith Park was wild, parklike only in the sense that the city owned it and the public was allowed in. Who knew what creatures roamed its depths? Halfway down she heard something large moving in the underbrush, coming closer, closer, then moving away. It smelled like a deer. Surely it was a deer.

All at once the view opened out onto the twinkling lights of Los Angeles far below. Closer by on her left a light in the neighborhood of the Krotona community showed red and pulsating. Odd how the austere Theosophists seemed to be staying up all night. Perhaps they were having a bonfire in honor of some heathen feast day.

The glow in the eastern sky was dying down and the stars were out when Emily came at last to the actresses' boardinghouse, exhausted and footsore. She could go no farther. Quietly, making never a creak, she lowered herself onto the porch swing, pulled her feet up, and fell asleep in the dark.

As the first light of day came up over the Hollywood Hills the thunk of a flung newspaper woke her. Emily sat up. Her hat was gone, her hair escaping from its pins, her clothes all wrinkled, torn and dirty, her shoes in rags. She was trying to smooth her skirt out with her hands when Gertrude Canty came out in her nightgown and wrapper to get the paper.

"Emily!"

"Gertrude."

"How—what are you—"

"I don't know. I don't know what's happening."

"Come in. I'm not dressed. It looks as though you aren't either." She brought Emily up to her room, along with the paper. Coffee was cooking on a hot plate. Wanda was still sound asleep.

"Come out here where we can talk." French doors led to a little porch furnished with a potted fern, two rotting wicker chairs, a twig tea table, and a startling view of the valley. The sun was rising on Los Angeles. Two cups of black coffee appeared on the table while Emily sat and composed her thoughts.

"We burned down Ross McHenry's house. Did you hear?" Gertrude said. She unfolded the paper, whose screamer headline read FIRE DESTROYS DOOMED STAR'S HOUSE.

"Good heavens. How?"

"Must have been Alma's spirit candles. We were halfway home before we saw the glow. How about you? What are you doing sleeping on the porch with your clothes all in disarray?"

"I was at that quarry, the one up in the canyon, the one with the cave. I don't know what happened. Holbert Bruns called the hotel and left a message last night for me to have Eddie Green drive me up there."

"Alone?"

Emily shrugged. How else but alone? "When we got to the quarry he made a heavy pass at me, and I jumped out of the car and hid in the cave."

"I wonder what you expected! Everyone knows what he's like! And then he drove off and left you up there?"

"I'm not sure. I heard a shot. The car drove away."

"A shot! I take it Mr. Bruns never showed up."

"Not that I know of."

"You think he—"

"Why would he use me to lure Eddie Green up there?"

"Why, indeed. If not to shoot at him."

"If not to shoot at him. For whatever reason. But then to leave me up there in the hills, in the middle of the night, alone, defenseless—you know, I used to think he rather liked me."

"I told you what you can expect from him. He's a Pinkerton man."

"Yes. I can almost understand about that. But to dump me on the side of a mountain—!"

"Holbert Bruns is not your friend. Holbert Bruns is your employer."

"Are you my friend, Gertrude? Even though I'm your employer? Because if you are you'll lend me some clothes and shoes. And a hat, maybe one of the ones I sold you in Flagstaff. I can't show up at the studio looking like this."

TWENTY-ONE

Emily arrived at the studio by streetcar, noticed the Cadillac limousine parked in the side lot, and made her way straight to the commissary, where she found Holbert Bruns coolly having his breakfast. Yesterday's *Examiner* was in front of him, open to Hester Mink's column. Sausage grease dropped from his fork onto the headline: MURDERED STAR IN SNOWBALL RING.

Emily slipped into the seat across from him. "I've been meaning to ask you, Mr. Bruns. What's a snowball ring?"

"I like your hat, Miss Daggett," Bruns said. "But I liked your other one better. In case you want it back, I left it for you at the hotel." His voice was cold.

"One can never have too many hats. What's a snowball ring?"

"I see where your friend Baby Wanda spilled the beans to that harpy from the *Examiner*."

"I wasn't aware that she had any beans to spill."

"She knew that Ross McHenry didn't commit suicide. That was all the Mink had to hear. Now she's trumpeting some poisonous story she picked up from a Japanese servant in the Hollywood Hills."

"You can't lay all the blame on Wanda. Don't you think Hester Mink was suspicious of the suicide tale to begin with? After all, something caused her to be up there poking around when Wanda ran into her. She must have known something wasn't right. What poisonous story?"

"The snowball ring story."

Mystified, Emily waited for Bruns to continue.

"She tracked down a houseboy who claims to have seen Ross McHenry in attendance at a number of weird homosexual drug parties. Clearly McHenry was killed by a member of the ring and thrown in the ocean, she says."

"She says that? In a family newspaper?"

"As much of it as you can say in a family newspaper. She didn't mention any names."

"Must be a pretty vague story, then, no names, no deeds. So that's what a snowball ring is. Is any of it true?"

"I had those tablets analyzed, Miss Daggett, the ones you found packed up in the case with the hypodermic syringe. Ross McHenry was an addict."

"I guess you think Eddie was supplying him with dope."

"Don't you? Isn't that why you—or were you defending your—"

"He says he was supplying the whole studio. He even tried to get me to take some. Was that why you wanted me to lure him up to the cave last night, the drugs?"

"I beg your pardon?"

"You telephoned the hotel yesterday and left a message for Eddie Green to drive me to the Union Rock Company quarry in Bryce Canyon. Have you forgotten? I had to walk back down the mountain, by the way. Spoiled a perfectly good pair of shoes. Thank you very much."

"Tell me something, Miss Daggett. Is there insanity in your family? Other than your own, I mean."

"I must have been insane to agree to work for you."

"I did not telephone and leave you instructions to get into a car with Chicago Eddie Green and drive to the darkest and most remote corner of Griffith Park. You knew how I felt about Chicago Eddie Green. How could you have believed I would do this?"

"How did you get hold of my hat?"

"Be quiet, Miss Daggett."

"What?"

"Can I make myself any plainer? Shut up."

After a long silence, during which Emily's face turned scarlet with humiliation, Holbert Bruns looked her in the eye and said, "Here's what actually happened, Miss Daggett." She waited, expecting him to explain himself. Instead of that he said, "Eddie Green drove you to the quarry. When you found that I wasn't there to meet you he drove you home again. End of story."

"End of story, good. But why—"

"End of story. Now we go and talk to Mr. Laemmle."

"I have bad news," Carl Laemmle told them. "Fortunately it doesn't reflect on the studio at all, but my chauffeur was killed last night. You remember Eddie."

Killed! Bruns somehow kept any reaction from showing on his face. Or he wasn't surprised. Or it wasn't news to him. Still he was ready to offer to do something about it: "You want us to—"

"No, no, the police are handling the investigation. As far as it goes. A simple case of robbery. The poor boy ventured into a bad neighborhood of the city last night and the criminal element shot him for the diamond in his ear. Never a good idea to wear flashy jewelry in the city. They found him in an alley this morning."

"But he wasn't killed there," Emily said, "someone dumped—" Holbert Bruns kicked her, kicked her really hard, his boots were quite thick and he broke the skin of her ankle, it made a bloodstain on Gertrude's best silk stockings. Shut up. Right.

"The police are handling it, Miss Daggett," Laemmle said. "Don't give it another thought."

"And the funeral—?" In a way she and Eddie had been friends. Surely there was some gesture she could make.

"His brother in Chicago is handling the arrangements," Laemmle said. "It's time now to begin planning *Captain Jinks of the Horse Marines.* Miss Daggett, how soon can you get me those dancing girls you were talking about?"

"So Eddie Green was the killer, he's out of the picture, and as far as you and I are concerned the case is closed," Emily said the minute she got Holbert Bruns alone in the hallway. "Is that how it is?"

"Yes," Bruns said. "That is correct."

"But he—"

"Miss Daggett, you have your hat, you have your picture to direct, your honor is still intact, or so I presume, and now our professional association is at an end." He took her hand and shook it stiffly. "I wish you the best of luck in your future endeavors."

"You're dismissing me?"

"Nothing personal. I'm moving on to an assignment with another studio."

"Oh."

"I've rented a small office downtown. As I think I mentioned, there's plenty of work in Los Angeles for an enterprising detective."

"Good luck to you, then, Mr. Bruns."

"I've enjoyed working with you, Miss Daggett, right up to the point where you—well, good-bye."

Her ankle still smarted. She watched him leave without asking about Eddie Green again, not only from a natural reluctance to suffer more physical abuse, but also from a fear that he might actually tell her the truth. For it was dawning on her that Bruns had shot Green himself and dumped his body in the city—frontier justice, Pinkerton-style, for killing McHenry; that he had returned the Cadillac to the IMP lot to distance the murder from the studio; and that he had taken the diamond stud to make it look like a robbery. Or worse, taken it to sell and enjoy the proceeds, Emily suspected, so low was her opinion of Bruns dropping.

TWENTY-TWO

No one from the police came to ask Emily what she was doing with Eddie the night he was killed, though she was perfectly willing to repeat the lie that Holbert Bruns had told her, how Eddie took her home and drove away. The image of Bruns ripping the diamond from dead Eddie's ear lingered in her mind and sometimes appeared in her dreams. She was not sorry when Bruns moved out of the Hotel Hollywood, and she did not ask him where he was going, or where his new office was, when she saw him leaving the lobby. She almost wanted to. She opened her mouth to greet him, but she saw the expression in his eyes. They nodded to each other coldly and moved on.

A week after Eddie's death the contracts were ready for signing. Emily and her troupe filed into Carl Laemmle's office on a glorious sunny afternoon. The Great Man had heard from Babette de Long's doctors, who had finally convinced him that his unhappy little star would not recover her wits in time to play Madame Trentoni for him, if indeed she ever recovered them at all.

"So this is the young lady you want for Madame Trentoni."

"Yes, sir. She has played the part on stage."

Gertrude gave Uncle Carl an even, affable gaze.

He stroked his chin approvingly. "Good," he said. "That will be fine. Sammy, draw up a contract for these lovely ladies, and also for—"

"Henry Gordon," Emily said.

"Who?"

"The boy from the morgue. You remember, his screen test was—"

"Right. Him, too. The name will have to be changed, make a note of that."

"What's wrong with my name?" the morgue boy said. "What's wrong with Henry Gordon? I put a lot of thought into it."

"No, this young lady's. Gertrude Canty. It doesn't sound right."

"So I should call myself . . . what?" Gertrude said.

"We'll work it out later. Blanche something, maybe." Mr. Laemmle told his nephew to see that the costumes and sets for *Captain Jinks* were in order as soon as possible, and to set up appointments for the girls with the studio hairdressers. "Nobody's name is right," he muttered.

"Nobody's hair is right. I want more blondes." He dismissed them with a wave of his hand.

"We should have a party," Etta said.

"We should," Emily said. And why not? She had everything she wanted from IMP now, and if she was not perfectly happy it was nobody's fault but her own. She was not perfectly happy. It was nobody's fault but her own. The abrupt defection of Holbert Bruns had left a surprisingly painful hole in her life. Had he really killed Eddie Green? Why wouldn't he speak to her? When was she going to learn to stop expecting good things from men?

"We're all movie stars now, thanks to Emily," Etta said. "I love it. This is so much better than being a detective. My only regret is that I never got to carry a gun."

"Being a movie star is all right so far," Wanda said, "but sometimes I think I might be tired of show business."

"How can that be?" said the morgue boy.

"I've been on the stage since I was two. Besides, I kinda liked being a detective. Fighting crime was fun."

"I'm sure Holbert Bruns will take you back any time you want to work for him," Emily said. "If you want to work for him."

"Why wouldn't I?"

"Self-preservation, for one thing."

"Aw, you know you're sweet on him."

"Am not."

"Are too."

"We should go to Feeny's and celebrate the signing of the contracts," Gertrude said. "Is it still padlocked?"

Wanda shook her head. "Still padlocked. I know what. Let's go to the Santa Monica Pier. We can get beer there."

Etta said, "Swell. We'll all go."

Wanda said, "Yes, and the morgue boy will be my escort, won't you, dear?"

"Henry. My name is Henry."

"Henry. Of course. You can bring your Mr. Bruns, Emily."

But, no; her Mr. Bruns was long gone. Instead of bringing him to the Santa Monica Pier, Emily brought the ghost of Chicago Eddie Green.

As the others danced and consumed hot dogs and beer Emily got on the carousel again, seeking the sensation of joyous detachment she felt the last time she rode it. But it was different now. The lights, instead of brightening everything, cast deep shadows. The faces of the painted horses were wild, demented. She saw Eddie's face in the crowd. He looked reproachful. Is that all? he seemed to be asking her. Is that it? Are you going to stop there? I thought you were a detective. You know me. Don't you know I didn't shoot Ross McHenry? Say, if I shot McHenry I'd still have had the gun when the dog got after me. I'd have shot it, too, before I let it chew my pants off. Wouldn't I?

Why don't we go for a walk down the beach and see Alma Kazanow?

Emily heard these words almost as if Eddie had murmured them in her ear, though afterwards she thought it must have been some sort of hallucination, induced by the delirium of going around and around and up and down to the music of the steam calliope. How she loved a waltz.

"I'm going to go for a walk on the beach," she said to Wanda, although Wanda and the morgue boy, dancing close, paid little heed to her. Gertrude, Etta, and Boris were nowhere in sight.

The noise and music of the Santa Monica Pier, the steam calliope, the band, the laughter and shouts of the children, the cries of the vendors, all faded in the distance as Emily retraced her path to the house with the tiled steps. A stiff breeze was blowing up, full of fog and wet stinging sand, threatening to unmoor her hat. Salt stuck to her lips. A bracing chill found its way under her clothes. Slowly her mental processes began to crank up, like the cold engine of a Hispano-Suiza.

Approaching the house from the ocean side seemed the best way, since Emily had no idea what the house looked like from the road. Even at that she might have been walking a completely different beach from the one she had walked with Chicago Eddie, so different was the experience. The tide was at its very ebb, the water out so far that she could scarcely see it in the dark and fog. No one strolled the beach now, not a soul in sight, and yet it almost seemed to Emily as though Eddie was still at her elbow, urging her on, his fear of dogs no longer of any concern to him. It was the strangest thing.

The moon gave off a watery light through the blowing mist, showing the tiles on the risers of Alma Kazanow's steps just ahead. The house was dark and quiet. If she wanted to, Emily could always let herself in. She still had the lock picks Bruns gave her. One thing she could never do again was visit Ross McHenry's bungalow. According to the newspapers there was nothing left of it. No one else would ever see the bloody mess in Ross McHenry's bedroom, or the clues in the drawer of his card table. No one else would ever smell his blood. Funny how a whole universe of sensations and possibilities, such as a furnished bungalow, could be there one day and gone the next, ephemeral as a moving picture set.

Ephemeral as a handsome young man. Eddie was gone. Emily knew that. Adam, the Adam she thought she knew for all those years, was gone, too. Let him go, God love him. The sand that crumbled under her feet seemed to slide toward the ocean. Everything was going west.

"I'm not well," Emily muttered. "Something is wrong with my head." The failure of her marriage to Adam had robbed her of her wits. She put her hand in her bag and touched the revolver. The very idea of shooting someone with it. Of shooting Adam. Sickness.

A figure came striding toward her out of the fog on the beach, draped in fringed garments that swayed first to one side and then the other, like a camel approaching across the sand.

"Hello. Miss Daggett, isn't it?"

"Mrs. Kazanow," Emily said. "How charming to see you here. Is this your house?"

"Yes, this is my little seaside cottage. Would you like to see it?"

"Oh, no, thank you, I was just passing by, taking a walk

on the beach. Such a beautiful evening." If you don't mind the chill and the fog.

"I insist. I'm so proud of it, you see; it's the first living space I've had that was all my own. How do you like the tiles on the stair risers?"

"I think they're quite enchanting. So original. Are they—did you design them yourself?"

"One of our group at Krotona is a potter. He made them for me. The motifs symbolize some of the guiding concepts of Theosophy."

"I see." The steps rose ever upward, not unlike the concepts of Theosophy, no doubt; Emily was almost out of breath from the climb by the time she reached the pinnacle of enlightenment, which was to say Mrs. Kazanow's porch, furnished with white-painted cast-iron chairs and a matching table. She turned and looked back out over the dark ocean.

"On a clear day you can see Santa Catalina," Mrs. Kazanow said. "But it's chilly out here. Come inside."

Like her quarters at Krotona, like Mrs. Kazanow herself, the living room of the beach house was draped in fringed paisley shawls. In the afternoon it must have been cheerful and sunny, facing west as it did with its big windows and glass door, but now it was dark as pitch. Mrs. Kazanow moved through the room lighting candles, lamps, and incense burners. The light of her match showed red through the flesh of her hand. Then as the candles blazed up, a soft glow illuminated the room, making visible the features of her face, her single eyebrow, the smoke of jasmine incense spreading in pungent layers.

"Won't you sit down?" she said. "I'll ring for some tea if you like."

"No, thank you," Emily said.

"But do sit."

Emily sat down at the card table, keeping the door in view and a tight grip on her handbag. Mrs. Kazanow took a chair opposite, with her back to the windows that looked onto the sea. Arranged on a chest next to where she was sitting was a collection of hand-thrown pottery glazed in dull blues and greens. She stretched out her hand and absently caressed the smallest of the pieces. Urn-shaped, it had a stopper in it.

"I'm happy to see you, Miss Daggett. I've been thinking of you."

"Indeed?"

"You came to my séance uninvited and threw beads at me. Why was that?"

"It must have been the house. I felt possessed by some antic spirit. If I ruined your séance I'm sorry."

"You are troubled."

"Me? Good heavens, no. My life is a bed of roses. All my troubles have passed."

"Nevertheless I feel it. Your aura is a very unhealthy gray color. Perhaps I can help. Allow me to do another reading for you. It's time, don't you think? So much has happened."

"Has it?"

"Oh, yes." She produced the cards, wrapped in a silken envelope. Where did she keep them? There seemed to be secret pockets in her gypsy clothes. She shuffled the pack, gave the cards to Emily to cut, dealt out the three cards, and turned over the first one, humming tunelessly. That first card, upside down, depicted a blindfolded woman dressed all in white, sitting on a bench with her back to the sea. Her arms were crossed over her breast. She held a long sword in each hand.

"The two of swords, reversed," Mrs. Kazanow pronounced at last.

"Yes." Emily could see that.

"This card stands for the strongest influence of your past. Ordinarily it represents sentiments which the sitter refuses to reveal, or to accept—are you aware of any such?—or a decision the sitter refuses to make, even a decision whose importance the sitter refuses to acknowledge. You have come to a crossroads. You must make a choice. If you close your eyes and think, you will understand the urgency of this choice. It is a difficult choice, this choice from your past. You may not have wanted to face it. Still, it remains to be dealt with."

"Of course," Emily said. Who didn't have unfinished business in her life? Good heavens, she could do these readings herself.

"Reversed, however . . . you see that the card is reversed . . ."

"Upside down, you mean. Yes."

"Reversed, the two of swords indicates that you have taken a decision, and in fact taken some action, but in the wrong direction. A card of lies, treachery, and dishonor."

"Dear me. Does the card say who was doing the lying?"

"This is a serious matter, my dear. It won't do to be flippant."

"It was a serious question."

Mrs. Kazanow ignored the question, however serious, and interrupted herself to light another cone of incense, sandalwood this time, in a small brass three-legged censer on the card table. More smoke trailed out of the holes. Emily stifled the urge to cough. Humming again, Mrs. Kazanow turned over the second card.

"Ah! The eight of cups. The influence governing your present." It portrayed a man with a staff in his hand, turning his back on the cups and walking away into the dark mountains. "An ending is approaching. The past is gone. What used to be true is no longer true. This card indicates that the sitter must accept the signs of change, no matter how reluctantly. The time has come for you to move on, my dear. You can see that, can't you?"

"Time to move on? I suppose so."

"This is a card of endings. Endings can be difficult. You feel weary, terribly weary. You will never be free of this weariness as long as you remain in California. A journey awaits you, a new life, but you must leave the old life behind. Bad things will happen if you try to remain."

"Yes." It was true that she felt weary. Her eyelids were heavy. Her head felt made of lead.

Mrs. Kazanow turned over the third card.

An armed skeleton on a white horse, bearing a black banner with a white flower and riding over the body of a king, over commoners, women, children. The card was labeled death.

"This is your future, Emily Daggett. Death, unless you change it. The cards say that you must leave California at once. Take the next train. Don't even pause to pack your belongings."

"My, my," Emily said. "Things look very black for me."

"I'm sorry. The cards never lie."

On the table was a blue-glazed bowl full of seashells. The light of the candle glittered on something among the seashells. What could that be? A bit of beach glass?

Or the diamond stud from Chicago Eddie's ear?

It was perfectly plain now who killed Ross McHenry. And who killed Eddie. Holbert Bruns did not kill Eddie, out of a sense of frontier justice or for any other reason. He found her hat in the Cadillac where she left it, next to Eddie's body, and thought Emily had killed him. Bruns must have moved the body to a Los Angeles alley to keep scandal away from the studio. No wonder he hadn't wanted anything further to do with Emily, a wild murderous woman, too dangerous to be around. That painful thing she saw in his face wasn't indifference, but disappointment.

Emily scooped up the cards, shuffled them, and handed them back to Alma. "Now you," she said. "I'll read yours."

"What?"

"I'll tell your fortune. Go ahead, shuffle them."

"I don't think—"

"You can do it, go on. Good. Now cut the deck."

Alma Kazanow gave her a strange look, but she shuffled and cut the cards as instructed. Emily turned over the first one, revealing the two of cups, upside down, lovers gazing into each other's eyes. "This is your past, Mrs. Kazanow," she said. "I see a dark bedroom."

"No, you don't," Mrs. Kazanow said. "That card represents—"

"I see a dark bedroom, two men in each other's arms,
and you in the doorway with a Browning semiautomatic
in your hands. I see you setting your dog on one of the
men as he goes out the window. I see you shooting the
other one where he stands, and after he falls to the floor,
shooting him in the head again and again."

Mrs. Kazanow stared at her, deathly pale. Behind her
Howie Kazanow in a bathing suit and bare feet silently
came into the house.

"I see you suborning your victim's own daughter to beat
what was left of his head in and carry his body away, telling her that it would save her mother from the gallows."
Still Mrs. Kazanow said nothing, but her hand went to her
neck.

"The second card," Emily said, turning the pile over to
reveal the seven of coins, a sad laborer leaning on his farm-
ing implement. "This would be the—what do you call it?—
significator for Chicago Eddie Green. I see you calling the
IMP studio and luring him to the quarry, waiting for him
there, killing him, driving the limousine back to the studio in the dark of the night. Taking his diamond earring
to make it look like a robbery. This earring." She plucked
the diamond out of the dish of shells and held it up. Howie
reeled backward, making a small sound. Still his wife
didn't notice him there.

"And now for your future." She turned over the third
card, which depicted a seated woman, blindfolded, holding a sword and scales. Was it coincidence, the tarot doing

its work, or the finger of a ghostly Chicago Eddie? For the name of the card was justice. "Justice. You must pay for your crimes."

"That diamond is mine. My trophy. Put it back."

Emily dropped the stud back in the bowl. "You found McHenry in bed with Eddie and you shot him."

"Not exactly in bed, but, yes, close enough."

"Then you set your dog on Eddie when he went out the bedroom window, and when the dog didn't kill him you lured him to the quarry and did the job yourself."

"It was easily done. You know, your boss's receptionist is an awfully stupid little thing."

"Everybody but you is stupid. Isn't that right?"

"It isn't that. You don't understand," Alma Kazanow said.

"Perhaps you can explain it to me."

"Ross McHenry was the great love of my life. He was mine. Do you know what that means? Mine. He didn't belong to his so-called daughter, or her mother, he didn't belong to those women in the movie houses, he didn't belong to those men in the bathhouses, or those silly dupes in the Krotona community, he belonged to me." She picked up the sealed urn. "He belongs to me still."

He belonged to her, so naturally she took his life. Killed her lover to keep him for herself.

Just as Emily wanted to kill Adam. Or not wanted to kill him, but wanted to keep herself from killing him, because the urge to do it was so strong. Was her heart like this woman's heart, a cesspit of selfishness and rot? She pulled Billie Burke's gun out of her bag and stared at it.

Only to think that just minutes ago she had wanted to use it on her own husband. The hammer was still cocked, the trigger sticking down.

Alma Kazanow noticed her holding it. "Spare me," she said. "Mine is bigger than yours anyway, as you can see." The Browning was in her bejeweled hand, aimed at Emily.

Behind her, Howie stepped away from the door. "Alma. No." Emily had forgotten him, standing so quietly. And still he might as well not have been there for all the effect his words had on his wife.

Now what? Emily pointed Billie Burke's revolver at Alma Kazanow, since that was what seemed to be called for. But what next? Put her under citizen's arrest? The publicity. Laemmle would be furious. "I guess this is what they call a Mexican standoff," Emily said. "I often wondered what was Mexican about it."

A low call rose from the deck outside. Alma Kazanow looked back over her shoulder and saw Howie watching her. And then, incredibly, Adam Weiss came strolling in, dressed in a bathing suit and robe. "Did someone mention Mexico? Oh, hello, Emily."

The world turned dark; the blood left Emily's fingers; the pistol, too heavy to carry now, fell from her hand onto the floor, where it went off with a bang.

TWENTY-THREE

"I think he's still breathing," Howie Kazanow said. "For God's sake, no police. If he dies we'll throw him in the ocean."

"We'll do no such thing," Emily said. "Go and get me a clean, wet towel. Hurry." There was blood everywhere. She tore a piece out of Adam's robe, how cross he would be, he probably had it custom-made, and began to clean his handsome face. By the time Howie returned she had found the wound; the bullet had clipped the top of his ear off.

She smoothed the hair out of Adam's eyes and blotted the gore from his eyelids. They fluttered open. "Emily. Is it you?"

"Yes, it's me, Adam."

He sat up, put a hand to his head, moaned. "I'm so sorry."

"It's all right."

"Will he be okay?" Howie said.

"He'll be okay. The top of his ear, a little bit of his scalp. He'll be okay."

"What happened?" Adam said.

"I was holding a gun on Alma, and you came in the door, and I dropped it by mistake."

"Why were you holding a gun on Alma?"

"She was holding a gun on me," Emily said. "She killed Ross McHenry, Adam. She killed Eddie Green. I'm surprised she didn't kill me. Where did she go?"

"My wife murdered two men," Howie said. "My God."

"You must have known, Mr. Kazanow," Emily said.

"Maybe I knew. Maybe deep down I knew. You're not going to tell the police, are you? Adam?"

Adam got to his feet unsteadily. "Me? No, Howie. It's just a little flesh wound. No doctors. No police." As always, Adam was perfectly willing to efface himself for his good friend Howie.

"Alma. Where did she go?" Howie stared through the window. "Oh, my God, she's walking into the ocean." He went out the door and down the steps, calling Alma's name.

And Emily was alone with Adam, the two of them face-to-face.

"Well, Adam."

"Well, Emily."

"I didn't mean to shoot you. It was an accident."

"Of course it was. Did you think I thought you meant to shoot me? I know you would never do that."

"I would never do that and miss you. If I meant it, there would be a little round hole between your eyes."

"Always the joker." Then he said, "I still love you, you know," and dropped to his knees in front of her, embracing her around her legs, burying his face in her belly, bleeding on her dress. "Emily."

She stroked his sticky hair. Here was her Adam returned to her at last. And yet. Did she really want him? What was it Mrs. Swaine said to her? Let him go. It's a mistake to try to breathe life into that which is truly dead. This feeling of numbness was very like death. Shocking how a scalp wound will bleed and bleed. Now it was all over her sleeve. "You should put a cold cloth on that," she said. "Where's Howie's towel?" Did she have to take him back now? What was the duty of a woman of honor in the twentieth century?

"I still love you, and I'm so, so sorry for all of this, but I have to ask you to sign some papers for a Mexican divorce."

"Really."

"Agnes and I are going to be married as soon as I get back to Ciudad Juárez."

"Best wishes," Emily said. "I would say congratulations, if the bride were anybody but Agnes. Where are these papers?"

Almost magically he had them in his hand, together with a fountain pen. "Agnes is a good girl. She's going to make me a father."

"Ah." She scrawled her signature in three places. That was that.

"A man has responsibilities, after all."

"So it would seem."

"Emily, Emily, God, how I want you. Share my bed tonight, one last time." For an instant the old hocus-pocus almost worked. She could feel the numbness dissipating. She could feel his warm arms, his face pressed into her belly, her own heart beating. How good it would be to share Adam's bed. How good it had always been.

But, soft. If she fell for this trick, Emily would forever afterward be the chorus trollop. For Adam really wanted nothing more from her than a bachelor party, some sexy fun the night before his wedding. A fine tradition for the groom, but surely not with his discarded wife.

"Why come to me? Why not get your friends to throw you a bachelor party? Howie probably knows some girls. Why not him?"

"What?"

"The two of you could get a little movie actress to pop out of a cake."

"Emily."

"Let go of me. You're bleeding on my dress."

As Adam reeled away from her the wolfhound came out of nowhere and pushed himself between them, making for the sea. Emily staggered backward. The dog went scrambling through the door and away down the steps.

Over the sound of the surf a shot rang out, followed by a howl of despair. Not the dog but Howie Kazanow was crying. He stood on the beach, staring out to sea, as Satan fought his way out into the dark waves. Alma was nowhere visible in the water. After a long moment Howie turned and came back toward the house, across the sand and up the steps, biting his hand, sobbing. The wet bathrobe dragged at his legs.

"What happened, old man?" Adam said.

"Alma walked into the ocean. She took that damned jar of ashes and a gun she got from somewhere. I tried to follow her, but I can't swim."

"She shot at you?" Emily said.

"She shot herself."

"Good heavens." Emily scanned the empty swelling waters of the black Pacific. No one was out there, no dead women, no dogs; nothing was visible except a few pale lines of foam where the waves broke against the sandbar.

"Don't tell anybody about this. You're not going to tell anybody, are you, Mrs. Weiss?"

"Miss Daggett."

"What?"

"Call me Miss Daggett, please." Adam stared at her, his jaw hanging slack. Perhaps he thought she should have been proud to wear his name. Perhaps he thought himself entitled to several wives. "I can't imagine who I would tell about it, Mr. Kazanow."

Howie bit his knuckles like a suffering movie hero. The poor man was convulsed by something, but was it grief or fear of adverse publicity? Emily couldn't resist slipping the knife in. "Except for Holbert Bruns, of course," she said.

"You're still working for him? I thought—"

"Oh, yes. Of course I'm still working for him. But have no fear; Holbert Bruns is a man of enormous discretion." She shook hands in a businesslike manner, first with Howie and then with the stupefied Adam. "Good-bye, Mr. Kaza-now. Good-bye, Mr. Weiss."

The look of pain and confusion on Adam's face as Emily bid him a cold farewell was delicious. She savored it all the way back down the beach, thinking, That's that then, now to forget him. As she drew nearer to the Santa Monica Pier the lights grew brighter, haloed in sea mist, and the music and laughter grew louder.

Almost without seeing it she crossed a wet trail that led up from the beach and into the bushes. The print of a long, thin slipper. The track of a dog. Afterward she remembered it and mentioned it in the report she wrote up for Holbert Bruns. Could have been anything, really. And that was that.